LIFE AND TIMES —AT— THE ROVERS RETURN

This book is dedicated to the memory of Alice and William Goodyear.

LIFE AND TIMES
—AT—
THE
ROVERS RETURN

ROVERS RETURN INN

SELECT · PUBLIC

DARAN LITTLE

B✺XTREE

Published in association with

GRANADA TELEVISION

ACKNOWLEDGEMENTS

The author and publishers would like to thank the following
for their help and support:

Julie Goodyear, Betty Driver, Beverley Callard, William Tarmey,
Sarah Lancashire, William Roache, Anne Kirkbride, Eileen Derbyshire,
Sally Whittaker, Michael Le Vell, Bill Waddington, Carolyn Reynolds,
Tom Elliott and Gareth Morgan,
and the man who created The Rovers Return, Tony Warren.

First published in 1993 by Boxtree Limited
Paperback edition published in 1994 by Boxtree Limited

Text © Daran Little 1993
Coronation Street © Granada Television
Photographs © Granada Television

3 5 7 9 10 8 6 4 2

A catalogue record for this book is available from the British Library

Design and typesetting: Anita Ruddell
Reproduction: Pica Colour Overseas
Printed in Portugal by Printer Portuguesa

BOXTREE LIMITED
Broadwall House
21 Broadwall
London SE1 9PL

ISBN 1 85283 907 4

CONTENTS

Foreword by Julie Goodyear 6

Early Years 8

Newton & Ridley 10

Spotlight on the Licensees 16

Ready and Willing 24

Six of the Best 52

How they Burnt Down the Rovers 74

Local Pubs and Landladies 80

Time Gentlemen Please! 88

What's your Tipple? 94

The Stars behind the Bar 98

Betty - Queen of the Hotpot 110

For the Love of Raquel 114

Jack's Glasses 116

The Queens - New Pub on the Block 118

Famous Faces 122

Tales from the Rovers 126

Roll Call 159

FOREWORD

CORONATION STREET is the most famous programme in the world and whenever anyone thinks of the Street they automatically mention The Rovers Return. It's the best-known pub in the world. I've been amazed when holidaying abroad to find the number of bars named after our very own pub.

The Rovers is the hub of the Street, the meeting place where the characters come together, gossip, have confrontations and celebrate. My very first appearance in the programme, in May 1966, was in the pub - machine worker Bet popped in for a pie and a pale ale.

When I first joined the cast of *Coronation Street*, the programme was dominated by superb actresses such as Violet Carson, Margot Bryant, Pat Phoenix, Doris Speed and Jean Alexander. I can still remember how awestruck I felt when I first ventured into the cast Green Room; all that talent in the one room! Little did I suspect that I would still be in the show long after those great actresses, and that my character would appear in more episodes than any of them!

Those actresses were wonderful to watch at work. I learnt so much from them. If I wasn't in a scene I would be hiding behind a scenery flat, keeping very, very quiet, hoping I wouldn't be thrown out of the studio, watching and observing all the different techniques and various mood swings of those fantastic actors and actresses. I was learning all the time. I wanted bits of them all and then I wanted to add my own style, something to personalise the character of Bet. I don't believe in imitation: I believe in originals. A lot of hard work and observation went into Bet and is still going into her.

I consider myself extremely privileged to have worked with some of the finest actors in the business and to have spent the last 23 years serving behind the world's most famous bar. Working with Doris Speed - the divine Annie Walker - was a sheer joy. Doris was a professional on screen and off. Under her motherly influence I gained confidence and experience. I will always be grateful for the help she gave me. When Annie left the series I was astounded, and delighted, when the producers told me that I was to take control of the Rovers. I can still remember the moment when brewery boss Sarah Ridley broke the news to Bet. "It's gonna change me life is this, isn't it?" was Bet's gutted reaction. It did!

For the past eight years Bet has run the Rovers, with and without Alec Gilroy. I still enjoy every scene in the pub and can't wait to open my scripts each week to see what Bet is up to!

I hope you enjoy this book. It's full of memories for me. Some happy - like Bet and Betty's antics behind the bar; some sad - like the tragic death of the marvellous Arthur Leslie.

It's truly an honour to play the landlady of The Rovers Return, and to welcome you to this celebration of my little domain.

Cheers!

Julie Goodyear

THE QUEEN OF THE ROVERS – JULIE GOODYEAR
HAS BEEN PULLING PINTS FOR 23 YEARS.

EARLY YEARS

"30 years ago there used to be a Black Maria outside Rovers Return every Sat'd'y night. An' coppers used to walk two at a time down Coronation Street. Annie Walker wouldn't o' lasted five minutes."

ENA SHARPLES

WHEN THE CAMERAS first rolled over the cobbles of Coronation Street in December 1960, the now infamous characters had histories dating back to their fictitious birthdates, giving them a reality unmatched in any other drama series. Like the characters, the Street itself had a history, interweaving the pasts of all the residents. In Episode Two, when Ena Sharples turned on Christine Hardman, reminding her that her mother had gone "pots for rags" and had been driven off in a little yellow van, the viewer could see years of conflict between the two characters. As she finished with weeping Christine, the formidable Ena turned on shopkeeper Elsie Lappin, telling her that she ought to be careful as the police were about the area: "It was the same story, durin' the war, with them ration books, wasn't it?"

Like all the houses in the Street, The Rovers Return Inn has its own history, dating back to 1902 when, along with the rest of Coronation Street, it was built.

The brewery was responsible for the building of the public house and had planned to name it "The Coronation" to celebrate the forthcoming accession of King Edward VII. However, they were forced to change their minds when the street itself was named "Coronation Street". Lt Philip Ridley, one of the members of the brewery-owning family, had recently returned from the Boer War and

the pub was given the name "The Rover's Return" to celebrate his safe homecoming. He was present on Saturday 16 August when the pub was officially opened. Later on, after the Great War, Lt Ridley had the pub name altered to read The Rovers Return (without an apostrophe) to celebrate the homecoming of all the local heroes. Jim Corbishley, a grocer by trade, was the first tenant in the pub. He had sold his Salford shop for £40 and took over the new pub with his wife Nellie and 17-year-old son Charlie. Charlie soon gained a reputation as a womaniser in the district and many local lasses fell for his charms. Sadly he died, aged 31, from injuries inflicted on the Somme. His girlfriend, barmaid Sarah Bridges was consoled by local rake Alfie Marsh. They shocked the neighbourhood by running off together and marrying bigamously. Jim and Nellie retired from the pub and bought a boarding house in Little Hayfield.

Retired police sergeant George Diggins took over at the Rovers in July 1919. His wife Mary struck a blow for women's rights when she served the local ladies in the Public as well as the Snug. The Diggins had no children, but Mary owned a small dog which slept in a basket made from a beer barrel under the counter. It lapped up any beer spilt onto the floor. The Diggins remained in the pub until 1937 when they moved away to Southport.

Newly-weds Jack and Annie Walker took over the pub in October 1937, having bought the tenancy from the brewery. Their children Billy and Joan were born in the pub during the blitz.

Annie Walker ran the pub more or less single-handed during the war while Jack served in the army. Annie had always wanted to use the pub as a mere stepping-stone to more gracious surroundings, and she had her heart set on a country pub in Cheshire. Jack, however, thoroughly enjoyed the time he spent behind the bar.

In the late 1950s the Walkers supervised the removal of the spittoons from the bar and replaced the sawdust on the ground with tiles. Realising that she was stuck with the pub, Annie had decided to make the most of the situation. On leaving school, Billy trained as a mechanic and did his National Service in Eden whilst Joan went to teacher-training college where she met Gordon Davies, the man she would eventually marry.

The residents of Coronation Street were almost as responsible as the Walkers for making the pub what it was by 1960 – a cosy hub of activity. Characters such as Ena Sharples and Albert Tatlock had drunk in the Rovers since the 1918 Armistice, whilst younger residents like Elsie Tanner and Len Fairclough had arrived in time for the Second World War and

had suffered, along with Annie, under Air Raid Warden Sharples. The 1950s had seen a younger generation grow up, including Dennis Tanner and Kenneth Barlow, both anxious – in their own ways – to change the world.

In the 33 years that *Coronation Street* has been screened, these characters have matured together and inevitably many have moved on, though there are always other characters to take their places, propping up the bar. These days characters as diverse as Percy Sugden, Rita Sullivan and Kevin Webster spend their evenings in the Rovers, exchanging views on topics, witnessing confrontations, consoling each other and having a merry time. In its 90 year history the little back-street ale house has always been a welcoming place, full of familiar faces and juicy gossip.

NEWTON AND RIDLEY

*"This brewery has always catered for the spit
and sawdust crowd."*

SARAH RIDLEY

IN THE SUMMER of 1781, Mr William Fairhurst formed The Stag Brewery in Weatherfield, a district to the south-west of Manchester, Lancashire. Fairhurst had trained as a maltster and been employed in a London brewery for twenty years. He moved up country, looking for financial backing to start his own business in the rapidly growing industrial city. At that time, Weatherfield was dominated by large cotton mills and factory dwellings. The Bridgewater Canal had been completed for nearly twenty years and Weatherfield, like its neighbours Salford and Castlefield, had grown overnight into a bustling, industrious

FAR LEFT: PERCY OAKES, THE LAST LINE OF THE OAKES FAMILY. TEN YEARS AFTER HIS DEATH THE NAME OAKES WAS DROPPED BY THE BREWERY AND IT BECAME NEWTON & RIDLEY.

LEFT: AUBREY NEWTON, THE DASHING BACHELOR WHO WAS THE LEADING INNOVATOR OF THE BREWERY. HE ROWED FOR HIS COLLEGE AT OXFORD AND ALMOST MADE THE 1890 BOAT RACE CREW.

town. In less than a decade, Manchester's population had doubled and the staple drink of every man and woman – and even the children – was beer. The average family spent more on ale each week than on any single household commodity. Here was an expanding market, just waiting for an entrepreneurial character like Fairhurst to exploit the opportunity.

Fairhurst interested local businessman Mr Fairley Oakes in his plans to produce high-quality beer at a reasonable price for the working man and woman. They built the new brewery on Bridgegate Street (now Albert Road), near the town's boundary with Manchester. Oakes' faith in Fairhurst proved well founded and Fairhurst's knowledge of beer served the brewery well. Whilst in London he had worked with saccharometers, the very latest technology for measuring the strength of beer, and he introduced the instrument at his own brewery – the first of the provincial brewers to do so. Oakes used his background in mill work to install steam power, rather than mill horses, to pump water and grind malt at the brewery. The mixture of saccharometers and steam power boosted beer production and quality, and The Stag Brewery soon established a reputation for serving beer of a consistent high standard.

Fairhurst died in 1824, leaving his share in the growing brewery to his partner, as he had no family of his own. Oakes, now in his early sixties, took his son Samuel on as his new partner and handed over the day-to-day running of the business to him. The brewing industry was changing dramatically – new systems of refrigeration and belt-driven machinery hugely increased production. Also beer duty was abolished in 1830, giving an extra boost to sales as home brews dropped.

The Swan Brewery had not tied itself to any outlets, as Oakes was reluctant to take on the financial burden of owning public houses. However, it was traditional for publicans to remain loyal to a single brewery and most of Weatherfield's ale houses sold Stag beer. Beer was delivered on credit; clerks from the brew-

THE DESIGN OF THE NEWTON & RIDLEY BEERMATS HAS CHANGED VERY LITTLE OVER THE YEARS. THIS LATEST DESIGN WAS FIRST USED IN THE 1950s.

ery visited publicans every month to collect payment for the balance sold. The abolition of beer duty led to a proliferation of beer styles and publicans found it hard to find breweries to meet all their requirements. Oakes, like many of his contemporaries, was compelled to buy public houses to safeguard his outlets. Most of the houses were not actually bought; rather they were acquired by Oakes from publicans who had fallen into debt and used their houses to pay off the money they owed the brewery for beer.

The Stag Inn on Bridgegate Street was the first public house to be built by the brewery. This was in 1848. That same year Fairley died and Samuel Oakes took control of the brewery, making his 18-year-old son Percival his partner. Two years later the brewery expanded its premises and a second house, The Flying Dutchman (later renamed The Flying Horse)

GEORGE NEWTON JNR OVERSAW BET'S TRANSFORMATION FROM BARMAID TO LANDLADY IN 1985.

was opened. Beer houses were on the increase in Weatherfield. In 1868, the Chief Constable reported that there were 206 of them in the town and that 74 beersellers had been summonsed that year for various infringements. One of them had his house closed for running a brothel on the premises.

The Wine and Beerhouse Act of 1869 forced beersellers to obtain a certificate from magistrates in order to renew their licences. The magistrates took the opportunity to close down many ale houses where the beersellers had disgraced themselves. The Compensation Act of 1904 allowed the licensing authorities to terminate any licence they considered unnecessary. The magistrates now closed houses simply because there were too many in the neighbourhood.

In 1879, Samuel and Percy welcomed two new partners – Aubrey Newton and Leopold Ridley. Newton, who had spent his whole working life at the brewery, had recently married Samuel's only daughter Joan. Ridley lived in the affluent Oakhill area of Weatherfield. His family, one of the oldest in the area, owned many of its factories and mills.

The turn of the twentieth century saw Newton, Ridley and Oakes open many of the public houses still found in the area. A network of residential streets had been built in the heart of Weatherfield and the brewery paid for public houses to be built all over the estate. The Rovers Return Inn on Coronation Street was opened in 1902, closely followed by The Crown and Anchor on Kitchener Street and The Tripe Dressers' Arms on Rosamund Street.

Percy, the last of the Oakes, died of a heart attack in 1904 and Newton & Ridley was formed, although they kept Oakes' name in the company until it was dropped completely in 1915. The brewery was still known as The Stag Brewery, although the house signs all displayed the name Newton & Ridley.

During the years of the Depression the brewery business suffered along with everyone else. The annual net profits shrunk by nearly 50% – to just over £50,000 in 1930. Guy Ridley took over as Chairman of the company the same year. He was also Joint Managing Director, a position he held with George Newton (Snr). At the same time the brewery suffered a blow when the Government put 2d on the price of a pint of beer. This increase led to a fall in consumption, reducing the national production of beer by a quarter. The Stag Brewery managed to survive despite this but was forced to sell off some of its houses. Still more were destroyed during the blitz on Manchester during World War II. If anything, these blows only strengthened the brewery: its beer was as popular as ever and the local people remained loyal to The Stag, despite an increase in tied houses belonging to rival breweries. Two of the company's directors, Hubert and Patrick Ridley, were honoured with Knighthoods after the War for their contributions to public morale: during the hostilities they had lowered the price of their beer and gave orders that servicemen would not have to pay for their first pint whilst on leave.

Cecil Newton, Aubrey's grandson, took overall control of the brewery in 1967. By this time the two families had been joined by the marriage of Cecil's sister Margaret and Sir

"BARMAID OF THE MONTH" TINA FOWLER IS PRESENTED WITH CHAMPAGNE BY NIGEL RIDLEY.

Hubert Ridley. The brewery became very much a family affair, with another sister, Anne, marrying Douglas Cresswell, who had served the brewery for 30 years. Cecil never married and he selected his board of directors from within the family – his brother George (Jnr) and niece Sarah Ridley dealt with the day-to-day running of the business in the 1980s. In 1990, Cecil retired and moved to Spain, although he kept his position as chairman of the board. Nigel Ridley took command of the company and oversaw many transformations in the public houses, encouraging tied houses to promote a wider range of drinks and turning

LEFT: WHEN TACKLED ABOUT WHY LIZ HAD BEEN GIVEN THE LICENCE OF THE QUEENS, RICHARD WILLMORE INSULTED BET BY SAYING HE LIKES TO MATCH THE PERSONALITY OF THE PUB TO THE MANAGERESS.

many into theme pubs. His greatest triumph was the transformation of The Riverboat on the newly developed Weatherfield Docks complex. However, a disagreement with Cecil about respect for the brewery's traditions led to Nigel's resignation. He was replaced, as tied-house manager, by Richard Willmore.

Willmore is known by the local landladies as "Tricky Dicky", a title given to him after only three months in office. He has a reputation for being a womaniser who sacks managers if they don't agree to dance to his tune.

Over 200 years have passed since Fairhurst arrived from London. The brewery has grown from an idea into a sprawling empire which covers Weatherfield and the towns around it. However, one thing has remained constant – the policy to produce good quality beer, reasonably priced, for the working men and women of Weatherfield.

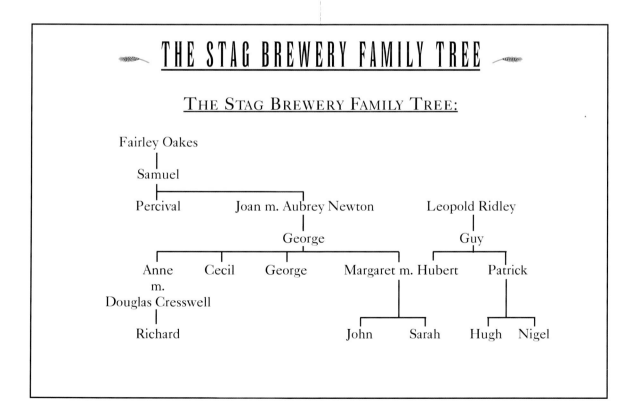

THE STAG BREWERY FAMILY TREE

THE STAG BREWERY FAMILY TREE:

Fairley Oakes
|
Samuel

Percival — Joan m. Aubrey Newton — Leopold Ridley

George — Guy

Anne — Cecil — George — Margaret m. Hubert — Patrick
m.
Douglas Cresswell

Richard — John — Sarah — Hugh — Nigel

SPOTLIGHT ON THE LICENSEES

*"I have been the hub of the community.
You might even say I have had my
own little kingdom"*

ANNIE WALKER

JACK

Full name: John Walker
Date of Birth: 26 April 1901
Marital Status: Married Annie Beaumont in
    1937
Children: Billy and Joan
Parents: Amos and Joan Walker
Last Address: The Rovers Return Inn,
    Weatherfield
First Appeared: Episode 2, 14 December 1960
Last Appeared: Episode 983, 24 June 1970
Number of Episodes: 807

Jack Walker was the first of the Rovers'
licensees in the series. Brought up in
Accrington (his father was a vet), Jack came to
Weatherfield in search of a job during the
Depression. He entered the licence trade and
took over the Rovers in 1937 with his bride,
Annie. During the War, he served in the
Fusiliers.

Jack was the backbone of The Rovers
Return, quietly observing the customers whilst
Annie was prone to ride rough-shod over them
in an attempt to lift the image of the Rovers
from working-man's ale house to sophisticated
cocktail bar. When Annie threatened to
become out of control he would gently, but
firmly, pull her down to earth by reminding
that, despite the pedigree of the Beaumonts,
she had been working in a cotton mill when
they met.

During his marriage to Annie, Jack came to
accept her inclination to over-dramatise a situation. Once, in 1964, she left him – mainly for
effect – when she suspected him of having a
mistress. The customers were amazed by Jack's
apparent lack of concern at the time. He
believed firmly that Annie would return once
she'd milked the situation for all it was worth.
He was right.

After Jack died of a heart attack in 1970,
Annie continued to polish his bowls trophies
with pride in her heart long after his death, as
no other man could replace her Jack.

FOR FOUR DECADES JACK WALKER RAN THE ROVERS. HE
WAS INJURED DURING WORLD WAR II AND WALKED WITH A
LIMP FOR THE REST OF HIS LIFE.

ANNIE

Full name: Anne Walker
Date of Birth: 11 August 1909
Marital Status: Married Jack Walker in 1937, widowed in 1970
Children: Billy and Joan
Parents: Edward and Florence Beaumont
Last Address: 4 Peacock Drive, Derby
First Appeared: Episode 1, 9 December 1960
Last Appeared: Episode 2351, 12 October 1983
Number of Episodes: 1746

Born in Clitheroe, Lancashire, Annie was the last of the Beaumonts, a family that could trace its origins back to William the Conqueror and whose motto was "We Shall Rise Again". Annie first moved to Weatherfield in the Depression and it as there that she met and married Jack Walker. They took over The Rovers Return Inn a couple of years before the outbreak of World War II. It was during the war that Annie took control of the pub and was forced beyond the confines of her sheltered upbringing, forging lasting friendships with the working people of Coronation Street.

Annie became a leading light in the local branch of the LVA and served as Weatherfield's last Mayoress. She was a woman of steel, who mourned the passing of the Empire and really believed she was a cut above the rest. Her sometimes vicious snobbishness often alienated her from her customers but they tolerated her for the sake of gentle Jack. But behind Annie's mask of hard landlady, she was a very vulnerable person. She had been hurt by her

Annie Walker tried to make the best of her years in a grimy back street. She once told potman Fred Gee how she coped every day: "I've been two people really: the landlady of The Rovers Return, and somebody quite different. Maybe that's made it bearable, especially since Jack died – being able to escape into my dreams."

children: Joan considered herself a cut above her pretentious mother and seldom visited her, and Billy constantly rebelled against the standards his mother strove so hard to uphold.

After Jack's death in 1970, Annie took over the licence of the pub and tried to educate her customers in the ways of the world. Annie herself was not educated but was fortunate enough to be a very good bluffer. She retired in 1983 and went to live with daughter Joan in Derby.

BILLY

Full name: William Walker
Date of Birth: 8 September 1938
Marital Status: Single
Children: None
Parents: Jack and Annie Walker
Last Address: Jersey
First Appeared: Episode 15, 21 January 1961
Last Appeared: Episode 2471, 5 December 1984
Number of Episodes: 408

Billy Walker completed his National Service in 1961 and settled down to the life of a garage mechanic. He probably would have done very well for himself in that business but for the interference of his mother, Annie, who kept trying to push him into the licence trade. She bullied him into taking more responsibility, but this backfired as he repeatedly fell into debt through gambling.

Billy roamed around the country through the years, occasionally returning home to show off his latest girlfriend. In 1974, he became engaged to local girl Deirdre Hunt, annoying Annie who found her too common. He took a job in Jersey when Deirdre broke off the engagement and made the island his home, running various clubs and hotels there.

When Annie retired she paid off Billy's considerable debts on condition that he took on the licence and ran The Rovers Return. His

name was above the door for less than a year before he crossed the brewery, fell foul of the law and was forced eventually to sell the Walker Empire back to the brewery.

ALEC

Full name: Alexander Gilroy
Date of Birth: 22 May 1935
Marital Status: Married Joyce Crosby in 1955, divorced in 1971. Married Bet Lynch in 1987, separated in 1992
Children: Sandra
Parents: Reg and Mabel Gilroy
Last Address: Southampton
First Appeared: Episode 1194, 26 June 1972
Last Appeared: Episode 3432, 2 September 1992
Number of Episodes: 522

Born in the back streets of Weatherfield, Alec entered showbusiness at an early age. He started running and managing clubs in the 1960s when his own theatrical career failed to take off. His first marriage was stormy and his wife Joyce eventually left him, taking their daughter Sandra to live with a footballer.

Alec learnt to be shrewd, mean and crafty as he clawed his way up the ladder in Manchester's clubland. In 1986, he fell for brassy Bet Lynch and surprised himself by the depth of his feelings for her. Shortly after their marriage, Alec was overjoyed when Bet conceived. Tragically, Bet lost the baby but the incident drew them closer together.

YOUNG BILLY WALKER WAS THE APPLE OF HIS MOTHER'S EYE. ANNIE WOULD HAVE BEEN MORTIFIED TO HAVE SEEN BILLY IN ACTION IN 1984, TRYING TO BLACKMAIL EMILY BISHOP BY THREATENING TO MAKE PUBLIC THE FACT THAT HER BEST FRIEND, DEIRDRE BARLOW, HAD HAD AN AFFAIR WITH MIKE BALDWIN, UNLESS EMILY GAVE HIM £6,000 TO BUY HIS SILENCE. LUCKILY, MIKE WARNED HIM OFF.

With his eye on the till and Bet charming the punters, the profits rose, although Alec always fought against spending anything, especially on extravagant Bet. Tragedy hit Alec once again in 1991 when, just after he had been reunited with his daughter, Sandra was killed in a car crash. Alec became guardian to his granddaughter Victoria, and struggled in his attempt to bridge the generation gap and become her friend.

Eventually, in 1992 Alec's theatrical roots caused the Gilroys to split. Bet refused to leave the pub when he was offered the job of a lifetime. Accusing Bet of wrecking their marriage, Alec left Weatherfield for Southampton where he now runs the entertainment programme for a cruise line.

BET

Full name: Elizabeth Theresa Gilroy
Date of Birth: 4 May 1940
Marital Status: Married Alec Gilroy in 1987, separated in 1992
Children: Martin
Parents: Patrick and Mary Lynch
Last Address: The Rovers Return Inn, Weatherfield
First Appeared: Episode 568, 23 May 1966
Number of Episodes up to June 1993: 1814

Brought up by her domineering mother – her father disappeared when she was just 6 months old – Bet rebelled against her staunch Catholic background and, by the time she was 16, she was pregnant. The baby was adopted but Bet had already gained a reputation for being easy, and the neighbours looked down on her as a willing tart.

Bet trained as a machinist and worked at various factories around Weatherfield. She fell in love easily, always with rogues who misused her and made her feel cheap. In 1970, she started work as a barmaid at the Rovers and continued her run of disastrous affairs, with men such

LEFT: ALEC'S THEATRICAL CAREER STARTED BY TRAINING FERRETS. HE PERFORMED AT WEDDINGS AND SOCIALS ALONG WITH HIS ELDER SISTER, EDNA, WHO SANG AND PLAYED THE SPOONS.

RIGHT: IN 1975, BET RECEIVED THE NEWS THAT HER SON MARTIN HAD BEEN KILLED IN A CAR CRASH IN NORTHERN IRELAND. HE HAD ONCE TURNED UP AT THE ROVERS BUT LEFT WITHOUT SPEAKING TO HIS MOTHER, UPSET BY HER BEHAVIOUR WITH THE MALE CUSTOMERS.

as builder Len Fairclough, factory boss Mike Baldwin and taxi driver Jack Duckworth.

Since 1985, Bet has run the pub. She married Alec because he offered security and was the only man to court her without pretending to love her. A year later she was devastated when she miscarried a baby. The incident brought back the heartbreak of the death, in 1975, of her only child Martin.

When Alec was offered a job in Southampton, Bet refused to leave the pub and her friends, so the marriage broke up. The Rovers is more than a pub to Bet – it is her whole life.

OVER THE LAST 33 YEARS MANY PEOPLE HAVE SERVED BEHIND THE
ROVERS' BAR. IN DECEMBER 1991, *CLASSIC CORONATION STREET*, A
PROGRAMME WHICH CELEBRATED THE SERIES, BROUGHT TOGETHER MANY
OF THE BARMAIDS FROM THE PUB, PAST AND PRESENT. HERE THE ROVERS'
LADIES TOAST THE PUB:

BACK ROW: ALISON DOUGHERTY, KATH GOODWIN, DOREEN LOSTOCK,
IRMA BARLOW (OGDEN), MARGO RICHARDSON, SANDRA STUBBS, MAUREEN
BARNETT, TINA FOWLER.

MIDDLE ROW: SUZIE BURCHALL, SALLY WEBSTER (SEDDON), GAIL PLATT
(POTTER), LIZ McDONALD, ANGIE FREEMAN, GLORIA TODD.

FRONT ROW: BET GILROY AND BETTY TURPIN.

READY AND WILLING

The Barstaff at The Rovers Return

*"Me behind a bar, I'm in me element.
I'm like Santa Claus in his grotto."*

BET LYNCH

ANNIE, JACK AND BILLY WALKER and Alec and Bet Gilroy have all held the licence at The Rovers Return Inn. Over the past 32 years these five people have run the pub with rods of iron – just ask anyone who has worked for them. A staggering 43 people have been employed at the Rovers over the years. Each has made a unique contribution, helping to turn the Rovers into the institution it is today.

BARMAIDS

CONCEPTA RILEY HEWITT

Irish Concepta was the first of the Rovers' barmaids. She was established behind the bar right at the start of the series, pulling pints for the likes of Harry Hewitt and Len Fairclough. Born in Dublin, Concepta had come to England in search of work and was taken in by the Walkers in 1959 as resident barmaid. Concepta was to become Annie Walker's most valued friend and companion. She respected Annie completely and was honoured when the older woman bestowed compliments on her. Concepta had a lot to put up with during her stint behind the bar. Although she worked hard, she was constantly criticised by bigoted Ena Sharples who referred

to her as "Paddy" and took every opportunity to run her down.

In October 1961, Concepta left the Rovers and married bus inspector Harry Hewitt. He refused to let her carry on working and for a time she devoted herself to looking after his house and daughter, Lucille. Financial trouble brought out an uncharacteristic stubborn streak in Concepta and she

CONCEPTA RILEY SERVING ONE OF THE PUB'S BEST CUSTOMERS, HARRY HEWITT, WHO BECAME HER HUSBAND IN OCTOBER 1961.

LOCAL LAD DENNIS TANNER WAS GLAD TO SEE YOUNG DOREEN BEHIND THE BAR. HER WIT AND HUMOUR BRIGHTENED UP THE ROVERS.

returned to the Rovers' bar part time. She left for good in 1962 to have a baby.

NONA WILLIS

Cockney Nona caused a sensation in the Rovers on her first night, in September 1961. Walking into the bar with her transistor radio blaring out, she received a cold stare from Ena Sharples in the Snug, who proceeded to tell her that Londoners were not welcome in her street. When asked if she had any bar experience, Nona naively replied "I've bin on the stage... exotic dancin'". With a sharp intake of breath Ena announced to the pub at large that Annie Walker had employed a stripper! Ena was not satisfied until Nona returned to the South two weeks later.

DOREEN LOSTOCK

Shop-assistant Doreen left her employer Leonard Swindley in the lurch to take a job at the Rovers, as Annie was offering £1 a week more. Unlike Concepta and Nona, Doreen was a local girl who was well known in the area. For a time she had dated Annie's son Billy, but, much to Annie's relief, the affair fizzled out. Doreen served in the pub for only a month, from October to November 1961.

IRMA OGDEN

Taken on part time at the Rovers in May 1964 (her main job was at the Corner Shop), Irma nearly lost her job on the first evening. To Jack Walker's horror she dropped Annie's Willow-pattern plate, smashing it into pieces. Jack rushed around trying to mend the treasured plate with glue, but eventually Irma confessed to Annie. To Jack's amazement, Annie thanked Irma for breaking it; she had never liked it.

When Stan Ogden's daughter Freda ran away from home, he went looking for her. Soon, however, tantalising reports of Irma, "the smashin' bit of cracklin'" working at the pub,

ON A VISIT TO SEE HIS PARENTS
BILLY WALKER WAS ENCOUR-
AGED TO FIND ATTRACTIVE IRMA
SERVING BEHIND THE BAR.

ward teenager into a con-
fident young woman. Part
of that time was spent
behind the bar where she
obliged Auntie Annie by
helping out. Lucille had a
variety of jobs, none of
which Annie thought
suitable. She was once a
Go-Go dancer and caused
a sensation by dancing on
the Rovers' bar top.

Emily was taken in by
Annie when she was
homeless; Annie thought
her a suitable companion
with whom she could dis-
cuss literature and art.

led him to postpone his search in favour
of a pint at the Rovers. He was surprised to find that the attractive new
barmaid who was causing such a stir
was none other than his lost daughter
– she had changed her name because
it sounded more glamorous.

Irma stayed behind the bar for six
months.

LUCILLE HEWITT AND EMILY NUGENT

Tearaway Lucille and teetotal
Emily both lived over The
Rovers Return in the late 1960s
and early 1970s.

Lucille was the Walkers' ward who moved
in when her father Harry Hewitt and step-
mother Concepta Riley emigrated to Ireland.
During her stay, she blossomed from an awk-

A MOST UNLIKELY BARMAID – EMILY NUGENT SERVES
AUDREY FLEMING.

Emily paid rent to the Walkers but she also felt obliged to serve behind the bar in her spare time. She was forced to stop the practice in 1970 when the Mission committee objected to their secretary serving in an ale house.

BETTY TURPIN

In the Summer of 1969, Annie spent a month holidaying in Majorca. Jack managed as best he could with the help of Lucille and Emily, but after a couple of hectic days he decided to take on someone full time. Betty had recently arrived in the Street and was lodging with her sister, Maggie Clegg, who ran the corner shop. Betty had experience of bar work and fitted in behind the bar with ease. To Jack she was a godsend, and she was very popular with the customers, but, unfortunately, Annie did not trust Betty. On her return, Annie felt displaced by jovial Betty and became jealous of her strong friendship with Jack. Annie told Betty she was no longer needed, but Betty refused to leave the pub; she maintained she was a good barmaid and one day Annie would be grateful to have her around. Twenty-four years later Betty is still serving behind the bar.

BET LYNCH

Billy Walker took on Bet as the new Rovers' barmaid one day when his mother was out

Miss Weatherfield 1955, Elizabeth Theresa Lynch astounds the menfolk with her outfit for her first night behind the Rovers' bar in November 1970.

18-YEAR-OLD GAIL POTTER WAS BROUGHT IN BY ANNIE TO HELP OUT DURING A CRISIS.

shopping in November 1970. Annie had decided that with Jack dead and Billy around to help out, she would take on the role of hostess, talking to the customers whilst her staff served. She would need another barmaid to help Betty, but one glance at Bet, in her body-hugging black dress and false eyelashes, was more than enough. She instructed Billy to give Miss Lynch notice straight away: "Am I biased or does her name sound as if it should be over a porn shop?". Billy refused to sack Bet, certain that Bet would prove an instant hit with the customers and that profits would soar. He was right. Within a week, Annie swallowed her pride and agreed that Bet could stay; she knew a good barmaid when she saw one. However, Annie remained amazed that grown men would fight to get Bet's attention. Cleaner Hilda Ogden announced to the pub at large "The day I have to look like that to attract the fellahs is the day I give up the struggle as a femme fatal."

Over the years, Bet proved worthy of Annie's faith in her. For the fifteen years she served under the Walkers, Bet gave herself body and soul to the Rovers. Perhaps her finest years were those in which she served with Betty and Fred Gee from 1976 to 1984.

Bet was always adamant that she was the main attraction at the Rovers, even more so than the beer. She once started a tips battle, forcing Betty and Fred to keep their own tips separate from hers. Behind the bar Bet set out a glass each for their expected tips: a pint pot for her own, a half-pint for Betty's, and a sherry glass for Fred's. Annie stopped the battle when it became obvious that Bet's campaign had degenerated into an ego trip.

When Billy Walker sold the pub back to the brewery in 1984, Bet was stunned by the regulars' suggestion that she apply for the post of manager. Backed by a petition from all the customers, Bet was taken on as the brewery's first single manageress and the first barmaid ever to win her own pub.

GAIL POTTER

Teenager Gail worked at the Rovers for only two days in November 1976, helping Annie out when Bet and Betty had walked out over a wages dispute. She was given the run-around by Bet who, as a customer, ordered exotic cocktails which Gail had no idea how to make. She was thankful to leave when Annie sorted out the difficulties with her staff.

DAWN PERKS

Following another dispute with Annie in 1977, Betty walked out of the pub. Annie knew she was going to absent herself for a time while she visited her daughter, so she advertised for a new barmaid to help Bet out. Dawn Perks answered the advertisement and, armed with

BET WAS JEALOUS TO SEE HER OLD FLAME MIKE BALDWIN MAKING A PLAY FOR DAWN.

ARLENE'S STAY AT THE PUB WAS CLOUDED BY THE IDEA THAT FRED HAD A MYSTERIOUS DISABILITY.

some inside information about how to impress Annie Walker, she was taken on. Annie was particularly delighted by Dawn's sober, respectable appearance – so different from brassy Bet. However, as soon as Annie left, Dawn emerged in her true colours – plunging necklines, short skirts and high heels.

Dawn proved a hit behind the bar and jealous Bet looked on as all her favourites asked to be served by Dawn. Bet knew she would have to take drastic steps to rid herself of Dawn and, after getting Betty to agree to return, sacked Dawn when she refused Bet's request for her to clean the toilets. Dawn marched off, telling Bet she was welcome to be "Queen of this flea-bitten castle".

ARLENE JONES

Relief barmaid Arlene served at the Rovers for just a week in 1980. She was employed by lecherous Fred Gee to help out while Betty was ill. Bet decided to have some fun, telling Arlene that she shouldn't take any notice of Fred's disability. Fred was puzzled when Arlene spent the week eyeing him cautiously, trying to fathom the nature of his problem. When he finally made his move on her, she fled.

DIANE AND CAROLE

Annie returned from a Mediterranean cruise in March 1981 to find relief manager Gordon Lewis had sacked her staff and taken on blousy Diane and Carole. She refused to let them stay and sent them, and Gordon, on their way.

SUZIE BIRCHALL HAD TWO STINTS IN THE PUB – STANDING IN FOR BETTY WHILE SHE WAS ILL, AND THEN FOR BET WHILE SHE WORKED AT THE CORNER SHOP WHEN HER LANDLORD, GROCER ALF ROBERTS, HAD TRIPPED OVER ONE OF HER SHOES AND FALLEN DOWNSTAIRS.

PULLING A PINT WITH A SMILE – KATH GOODWIN STOOD UP FOR BARMAIDS' RIGHTS.

SUZIE BURCHALL

Suzie was taken on at the Rovers after telling Annie she had served in all the best London bars. Annie knew she was lying, but with Betty ill, she was short-staffed and desperate. She was surprised when Suzie proved to be a very good barmaid. Suzie even survived jealous Bet's attempt to get rid of her: Bet told Vera Duckworth that her husband Jack had taken Suzie out. Vera gave Suzie a mouthful of abuse in the Rovers, only to have Suzie calmly tell her she wouldn't touch Jack with a barge-pole. Bet was stunned when Annie commended Suzie for the way she had dealt with Vera.

KATHY GOODWIN

Brought in to help out in 1984 by acting-manager Fred Gee, Kathy was quick to realise that Fred fancied his chances with her. Fred offered to take her to a brewery dance and she agreed before discovering that he had already asked Bet, who had also agreed. Fred was adamant that he wanted Kathy rather than Bet, but Kathy refused to upset Bet. The matter was complicated further when Fred was taken ill and replaced by Frank Harvey. Frank also asked Kathy to be his guest, but again she refused. Frank pulled rank on Bet and ordered her to accompany him, but Bet struck a blow for barmaids when she arrived for the dance dressed as a tramp.

MAUREEN BARNETT

In January 1985, Bet was made manager of The Rovers Return. While she was away on the training course, Frank Harvey was called in again to run the pub. Betty didn't trust him to find suitable help, so she employed her friend Maureen to assist behind the bar for a couple of weeks until Bet returned.

GLORIA TODD

Bet Lynch returned from her management training course to find a new barmaid in the pub. Gloria had been taken on by Frank Harvey, although it was obvious she had no experience of bar work. Bet sacked her after a day, prompting Gloria to accuse her of being jealous of her youth and of not being able to stand the competition.

Six months later Gloria returned, this time with experience and maturity gained by having served in one of the brewery's roughest pubs. Bet welcomed her on board after she quickly proved her worth. Ironically, Gloria was to become one of Bet's closest friends. When Bet married Alec Gilroy in 1987, Gloria attended her as her bridesmaid.

Gloria searched for love but always attracted the wrong sort of man: Alan Bradley two-timed her with Rita Fairclough, Frank Mills made a violent pass at her, Steve Holt haunted her on his release from prison, Mike Baldwin used her as a cover for his affair with a married woman, and Jack Duckworth sent her anonymous roses. Gloria left the Rovers in November 1988 after declaring her love for the boyfriend of cleaner Sandra Stubbs.

AFTER HELPING TO SAVE THE PUB FROM BURNING DOWN,
SALLY JOINED THE STAFF.

BET RECRUITED ALISON DOUGHERTY IN BETTY'S HOUSE.

ALEC PRESENTS NEW BARMAID MARGO
RICHARDSON TO A DOUBTFUL GLORIA.

SALLY SEDDON

Chirpy Sally was employed by Bet to help give
the Rovers a new image when it was reopened
after the fire in 1986. Sally was delighted to
have the job as she was saving up
to marry Kevin Webster, but she
walked out a month later when her
hours were cut by Bet.

ALISON DOUGHERTY

Along with Sally, Alison helped
Bet behind the bar when the
Rovers was reopened. However,
she was poached by Bet's rival Alec Gilroy after
her first day. He employed her at The Graffiti
Club but she disappeared with the takings after
two days.

MARGO RICHARDSON

When Bet ran off to Spain in the summer of 1987, Margo was taken on by acting-manager Alec Gilroy. She worked hard behind the bar, surprising Betty who thought she looked like a Christmas tree – all tinsel. When Bet returned, engaged to Alec, her first step was to sack Margo to whom she took an instant dislike.

TINA FOWLER

Bet employed Tina when she needed a barmaid in March 1989 because she recognised many of her own qualities in the sparky young woman. Straight-talking and a wisecracker, Tina soon sorted out the amorous regulars. Jack Duckworth made a big play for Tina and finally, to teach him a lesson, she agreed to go out with him. She allowed him to spend a fortune on her before giving him a quick peck on the cheek and disappearing into the night.

Tina caused a fight in the Rovers when builder Eddie Ramsden pestered her for a date. She refused and was upset by his leering remarks, but Kevin Webster stood up for Tina and a fight broke out. To everyone's amazement she then agreed to go out with Eddie and before long they were engaged to be married. Tina was stunned when Eddie told her during her hen party that he intended to marry someone else, but she quickly bounced back, slicing up her wedding cake for the regulars.

Tina started to get ideas above her station when she dated brewery boss Nigel Ridley. She barred Percy Sugden from the Rovers because he bored her by talking about the War. Bet sacked her on the spot.

LIZ McDONALD

Liz replaced Tina in September 1990. Alec was wary of employing her at first as he feared her husband Jim would be too possessive and might cause trouble if customers tried to chat her up. He was won round when Bet pointed out that Jim was a big drinker and it would help trade to have him in the pub every session keeping an eye on his wife!

VERA DUCKWORTH WAS FURIOUS TO DISCOVER TINA HAD HUMILIATED HER HUSBAND JACK.

WHEN HE HIRED LIZ McDONALD, ALEC WAS WARY OF HER HUSBAND JIM.

RAQUEL TOOK LONGER THAN MOST TO LEARN THE SKILLS OF BARKEEPING.

RAQUEL WOLSTENHULME

Raquel became the 24th Rovers barmaid in January 1992. A model by profession, Raquel is quick to point out that she only works at the pub between assignments, although she only seems to get jobs modelling slippers. Raquel moved into the Rovers' spare room after a failed romance with Des Barnes. She quickly forgot Des when she met County football star Wayne Farrell. She became the butt of the regulars' jokes when she continued to be unaware of Wayne's infidelities and failings as a footballer, although it was obvious to everyone else exactly what was going on. Finally, County's press officer Gordon Blinkhorn forced Raquel to face reality when she confronted Wayne with one of his other women. Raquel has always been attracted to sportsmen and with Wayne out of the picture she was pleased to discover Gordon plays cricket.

Liz left the Rovers for five months as she recovered from the death of her one-day-old daughter Katharine. She returned in May 1992 to help cook food when the Rovers started to serve evening meals. When Bet took a holiday in 1993, Liz was given a chance to manage the Rovers. Brewery chief Richard Willmore felt she was good landlady material and encouraged her to apply for her own pub. In May 1993 she was made manageress of The Queens, the brewery's show-piece pub.

ANGIE FREEMAN

Design student Angie helped out in the evenings at the Rovers over Christmas 1991. At the same time, her boyfriend Des Barnes dumped her for Raquel Wolstenhulme. Then Angie was no longer needed at the pub when the Gilroys took on a full-time barmaid – Raquel. Angie was furious that Raquel had taken her place once more and threw her shoes at her in the pub, saying she might as well have them as well!

REVENGE IS SWEET – ANGIE THROWS A PINT OF BITTER IN DES BARNES' FACE.

MANAGERS

Although only five people have held the position of licensee of The Rovers Return, there have been a handful of managers who have looked after the pub – and kept an eye on the staff – during their absences. Most of the Rovers' managers have been ambitious and have cast covetous eyes over the pub's licence.

Bet is now manager of the bar since Alec sold the tenancy back to the brewery when he left for Southampton in 1992. It has taken some time for her to adjust to not being her own boss any more.

VINCE PLUMMER

When Jack and Annie Walker took a holiday in the Summer of 1961, the brewery sent Vince to run the Rovers. He upset the customers immediately by making sexual overtures towards barmaid Concepta Riley. When her boyfriend Harry Hewitt warned him off, Vince told him not to be so possessive and

LONDONER VINCE PLUMMER UPSET THE REGULARS BY MAULING CONCEPTA RILEY.

pointed out that he would have no way of knowing what went on after-hours at the pub as both he and Concepta lived in.

When the Walkers returned, Vince told them he'd written to the brewery advising them that the Walkers and the Rovers were outdated and the whole pub needed shaking up. Thankfully, the brewery did not agree.

BRENDA RILEY

In 1966, Jack and Annie took a holiday in Ireland with the Hewitts, but they left their ward Lucille behind with relief-manager Brenda. Irish Brenda was a hit with the customers, making the menfolk comfortable in the bar and her new living-quarters.

GOOD-TIME BRENDA CAUSED A SENSATION AT THE ROVERS AMONG THE MENFOLK.

She encouraged Lucille to experiment with make-up and threw after-hours parties for the regulars. The Walkers returned after three weeks to find a snooker tournament in progress in the pub and Lucille dancing on the bartop. Annie threatened to report Brenda, but Brenda announced she'd had enough of the licensed trade. She left the area with engineer Jim Mount, who had plans to become her fifth husband.

ARTHUR WALKER

The one manager Jack Walker felt he could trust was his brother Arthur. Arthur ran his own pub, The Nag's Head, and he and Jack took it in turns to deputise for each other. Arthur looked after the pub in November 1969 whilst the regulars went on a coach trip to Windermere. The outing ended in disaster when the coach crashed.

WHILST JACK REMAINED IN HOSPITAL, ARTHUR HELPED ANNIE SERVE THE OTHER CRASH VICTIMS.

BILLY WALKER

Years before he held the licence, Billy ran the Rovers as manager. His mother Annie was made Mayoress in 1973 and she handed the running of the pub over to Billy. He was a heavy gambler and borrowed money from the till to fuel his passion. When Annie discovered this, he was forced to confess to being £200 in debt; Annie took back control of the pub and handed him a personal cheque to cover the debt.

BILLY CAUSED HIS MOTHER NO END OF HEARTACHE. HE NEVER SHARED HIS FATHER'S LOVE OF THE ROVERS.

GLYN THOMAS

Welsh Glyn replaced Billy as manager in June 1973. The regulars were amazed when Annie stood back and let Glyn make sweeping changes in the pub. He attempted to bring in fresh trade by laying on functions in the Select: pop groups and a lady organist entertained customers who paid money to enter the room and an extra few pence for drinks. To avoid breakages, Glyn ordered plastic glasses and he pushed Betty and Bet into the kitchen to see what they could cook up to sell over the bar. He moved a jukebox and a fruit machine into the Public Bar and played piped music in the Snug. The regulars complained that their quiet, friendly local had turned into a loud,

BET TRIED TO GET ROUND GLYN BY WAY OF HIS STOMACH.

WHEN GORDON LEWIS TOOK OVER IN 1981 A CLASH OF WILLS RESULTED IN FRED'S SUSPENSION.

cold club overnight.

Annie decided to retire and leave the pub in Glyn's hands for good. The regulars found out and begged her to stay, presenting her with a petition from them all. She was genuinely touched by their affection and concern, and she agreed to stay. The brewery moved Glyn on and Annie reclaimed her Select. One legacy of Glyn's reign did remain – Betty's hotpot proved so successful that it was kept on the menu and remains there to this day.

GORDON LEWIS

In March 1981, Annie booked herself onto a cruise. Not trusting her staff, she asked the brewery to send a relief-manager to run the pub. As soon as she was out of the way, Gordon Lewis turned off his golden smile and showed his true colours. He reprimanded Bet for pulling a pint for Len Fairclough out of licensed hours when he was working in the pub; he publicly humiliated Betty by ticking her off when Stan Ogden accused her of short-changing him; and he suspended Fred for helping himself to the optics. Bet and Betty walked out in support of Fred, and Gordon brought in two rough barmaids, Carole and Diane, to help out. Annie returned to find her pub being run by strangers. When she tackled Gordon about the situation, he told her she was too lax with her staff and that she was too old to run a pub.

Annie pulled rank and informed the brewery of Gordon's impertinence. He was removed straight away.

Three years later he returned. This time he promised Bet and Betty there would be no conflict; he was in charge. With Annie retired and the brewery looking for a permanent manager for the pub, Gordon applied, telling Sarah Ridley his plans for the pub – knocking the pub through into just one bar, with the front door on Rosamund Street, a main road. Gordon was confident he had won the pub and was stunned when the brewery gave the post to Bet. He was moved to a dockland pub notorious for its rough clientele and stabbings.

FRED GEE

When Fred became potman at the Rovers in 1976, he confessed to Annie that he had ambitions to run his own pub. She told him that the experience he would gain at the Rovers would prove invaluable. Fred's big chance finally came in 1984 when Annie retired. The brewery gave him the oppor-

DURING HIS BRIEF REIGN AT THE ROVERS, FRED CHANGED THE PIES AND EMPLOYED KATH GOODWIN.

BET WAS ALARMED TO DISCOVER FRANK HARVEY BACK IN THE PUB WHEN SHE BECAME MANAGERESS.

tunity to prove his worth by putting him in charge of the Rovers. Donning a cravat, jacket and cigar, Fred mingled with the customers while his minions, Bet and Betty, served on.

Fred tried to gain a reputation for good pub-grub but wanted to save money at the same time. He ordered cheaper, inferior pies and tried to disguise the taste with garnish and pickles. When he collapsed behind the bar, the regulars felt certain he'd fallen foul of his own pies, but he was diagnosed as having acute appendicitis and was forced to give up the pub after only two weeks.

FRANK HARVEY

Lecherous Frank replaced Fred as manager just after Fred had taken on a new barmaid, Kathy Goodwin. Frank also inherited an invitation to a brewery dance. Fred had invited Bet to be his guest, but Frank refused to take her, preferring Kathy. Kathy refused to go in case she offended Bet, and when he eventually asked Bet, she refused to go on principle. Frustrated, Frank ordered Bet to go with him "or else!". Bet meekly obliged and went off to get ready. Having squeezed himself into a dinner jacket, Frank waited for Bet to arrive. When she did turn up, she was dressed as a tramp. Frank was furious and went to the dance alone.

He left the Rovers for pastures new in May 1984, but returned the following January to look after the pub while Bet went on a manager's course. He employed Gloria Todd, whom he had met in a club, and he lured her into his bed on her first night. Betty was glad to see the back of him when Bet returned.

BET GILROY

Bet became the brewery's first single manageress in January 1985, when she was still Bet Lynch. When she was given the news by Sarah Ridley, her first reaction was "this is gonna change me life, is this". She was right: slowly, Bet matured from a dizzy barmaid out for a good time into a responsible, perceptive landlady. In 1987, Bet bought the licence from the brewery for £15,000, using money borrowed from Alec Gilroy. However, after only two months Bet found it impossible to make the repayments and, rather than ask for help, she disappeared and flew to Spain, where she took a job in a café. Eventually Alec tracked her down, brought her home and married her. They ran the pub together until Alec left to live in Southampton in September 1992. Bet now runs the pub as manageress once again.

BETTY TURPIN

At various times in the 1980s, Betty ran the Rovers while the landlords were away. In 1985, Bet returned from a holiday with Frank Mills to discover that the brewery (who hadn't been

AFTER 15 YEARS UNDER ANNIE WALKER, BET FINALLY TOOK OVER THE ROVERS IN 1985.

informed of her absence) had made Betty manager. Betty was in the uncomfortable position of keeping control of the pub while Bet was placed on probation.

LIZ MCDONALD

Given the free use of a villa in Tenerife in 1993, Bet Gilroy tried to get a relief-manager from the brewery to cover for her. The brewery had no one available at short notice, but they approved her choice of barmaid Liz to run the pub. Brewery boss Richard Willmore felt that Liz would make an excellent manager and she duly moved into the pub with husband Jim. Liz enjoyed running the bar and impressed the customers with her efficiency, though Raquel felt the new-found power had gone to Liz's head. When Jim gave up his security job they applied to Willmore for their own pub. Bet returned from holiday to the stunning news that her barmaid was to have a pub of her own.

RAQUEL WOLSTENHULME FELT THE POWER HAD GONE TO LIZ'S HEAD WHEN SHE TOOK OVER AS TEMPORARY MANAGERESS OF THE ROVERS.

CELLARMEN, POTMEN AND BARMEN

Newton & Ridley regulations state that the keeping of the cellar is one of the most important functions in their houses. Jack Walker kept a tidy, well-ordered cellar, and whilst he was alive Annie received no complaints from the customers. Billy ran the cellar when he managed the pub, but in 1976 the brewery insisted Annie hire a cellarman, Fred Gee. Since then various barmen have prided themselves on the ale served from their cellar. As well as cellarmen and barmen, potmen have occasionally been employed at the Rovers, their job being simply to collect used "pots" or glasses and sometimes to serve at the tables.

IVAN CHEVESKI

Polish Ivan was Elsie Tanner's son-in-law and he spent many evenings in the Rovers with

HARDWORKING IVAN CHEVESKI SPENT HIS DAYS AT THE STEEL WORKS AND HIS EVENINGS WAITING ON TABLES AT THE ROVERS.

wife Linda, even though the couple lived in Warrington, where Ivan was employed in a steel works. In 1961, he agreed to buy No. 9 Coronation Street so that Linda could be near her mother. To help raise the deposit, he took an evening job at the Rovers, collecting glasses and waiting on the customers in the Select. The couple moved into the Street in May and Ivan continued to work in the pub up until they emigrated to Canada in December of the same year.

SAM LEACH

Mystery-man Sam arrived in the Street as a vagrant. Jack Walker took an instant liking to him and took him on to collect glasses. Sam lodged at the pub, and in his spare time he helped out the residents with odd jobs. He

JACKO FORD

Jacko lodged at the corner shop where his daughter Norma worked. Known locally as a petty thief and villain, he came to the Street after a long stretch at Strangeways. Billy Walker employed him as potman in July 1972, but he did not stay long: Jacko was identified as a thief by Betty Turpin, whose husband was a policeman. She refused to work with a criminal, so Billy set about proving to her that Jacko was reformed. He left £3 under the hall telephone as a trap for Jacko, certain that Jacko would not touch the money. He was proved right; Jacko found the money but did not steal it. However, he accused the regulars of trying to trap him and resigned from the pub rather than work where he wasn't trusted.

FRED GEE

Fred Gee buried his wife Edna in October 1975, after she had died in a fire at the warehouse. Less than a year later, he moved into the Rovers as resident cellarman. At the time, Annie believed him to be a timid, polite and respectable man who deeply missed his wife. Bet Lynch took an instant dislike to Fred, telling Betty she didn't trust him – he seemed shifty. Bet was soon proved right as Fred's true character became apparent – loud-mouthed, crude, self-opinionated, bigoted, chauvinistic and coarse. After a year serving with Fred, watching him chat up every female customer, Bet announced "There are only two sorts of women to Fred – propositionable and dead".

Fred always had ambitions to run his own pub. To that end he set about finding a wife who would be an asset behind a bar. He proposed to most of the barmaids he came across – including Bet and Betty! The only one to accept him was Eunice Nuttall, who had given the trade up to work in a dry cleaners. Fred discovered why she had given it up – she had been sacked under suspicion of theft and had

PROVIDING EXTRA SERVICE IN THE SNUG – SAM LEACH MADE PLENTY OF FRIENDS DURING HIS TIME IN THE STREET.

soon gained the reputation of a good samaritan and lay-preacher Leonard Swindley was asked to propose him for a "good neighbour" award.

Sam would probably have stayed in the Street if it had not have been for a old neighbour of his from Newcastle who recognised Sam. He told the regulars that Sam's nagging wife had disappeared and he was suspected of having murdered her. Annie Walker was shocked to discover she has giving shelter to a murderer. The next day the police arrived looking for Sam, but he had already disappeared. Annie was relieved to discover that Sam was only wanted for deserting his wife, not for killing her.

TO BETTY AND BET, FRED GEE ALWAYS REMAINED A JOKE AND FIGURE OF FUN.

JACKO FORD STORMED OUT OF THE PUB WHEN BILLY'S TRICK TURNED SOUR.

been blacklisted by the brewery. Unfortunately for Fred, he didn't find this out until after he had married Eunice. This was in May 1981 and by the end of the year they had separated.

In his attempts to win a woman, Fred went to great lengths. In 1979, desperate to attract Audrey Potter, he donned a wig. Annie was horrified by the sight of Fred's new mop but no one could bring themselves to pass comment on it, until pensioner Albert Tatlock told an embarrassed Fred that he looked "a complete idiot"; Annie found the wig in her dustbin the next day.

Annie often had to issue warnings to Fred over the frequent brawls he got into in the bar. One even spilled over into her living room, with Fred scratching her treasured sideboard. On that occasion, as in many others, Fred was fined out of his wages for the inconvenience he

had caused Annie. Questioned on why Annie employed loutish Fred, she answered that she felt sorry for him and looked upon it as a charitable act.

When Annie retired from the pub, Betty and Bet were horrified that the brewery automatically gave command of the pub to Fred because he already lived in, and was, furthermore, a man. Fred's reign was short (see MANAGERS) and he finally left the pub for good in the Summer of 1984, after he thumped new licensee, Billy Walker.

WILF STARKEY

When Bet Lynch took command of The Rovers Return, the first thing she realised was that she would need a good cellarman: apart from the fact that she intended to be always present behind the bar, she also hated going down the spider-ridden cellar. Wilf Starkey offered his services before Bet had advertised. She was impressed by his references and told him the job was his. She was taken aback when he informed her that he would give the pub a trial and stay on if it came up to scratch. Wilf soon decided he and the Rovers were ideally suited.

He told the male customers that he had Bet and Betty hanging on his every word. However, Bet soon showed him – and the customers – who was in charge when she saw off two thugs who had caused trouble at the pub and had frightened Wilf!

Bet was faced with a dilemma in the Summer of 1985, when a customer had died in a car crash after drinking at the pub. Before he died he had left his brief-case, containing £4,000, at the Rovers. Wilf found the bag and pocketed the money. Bet was faced with a police and brewery investigation over the missing money and confronted her staff. Wilf broke down, confessed all and returned the money untouched. He told Bet he didn't know what had come over him and had been unable to stop himself. Bet decided not to inform the police, winning Wilf's gratitude. However, the die was cast and Bet could no longer trust Wilf. He walked out of the pub in August 1985 when Bet discovered that the till was down by £5. After he had gone, Ken Barlow returned the money, telling Bet he'd been given too much change.

FRANK MILLS

Wilf was replaced by Frank Mills, a man who knew how to exploit his charms. He came to Weatherfield looking for work in upmarket cock-tail lounges. He had previously met Bet when she holidayed in Blackpool and she gave him lodgings at the Rovers. In return, he showed off his skills behind the bar. Bet recognised Frank as an asset, and he told her he would work full-time for her if his domestic conditions improved. Admiring his cheek and charm, Bet agreed to his conditions and let him into her bed. But Frank was not content and his roving eye settled upon barmaid Gloria Todd. He made a pass at her and became violent when she resisted him. Gloria told Bet and she showed him the door on New Year's Day 1986.

JACK (LEFT) AND CHARLIE (ABOVE)
BOTH SERVED AT THE SAME TIME. HOWEVER STELLA
RIGBY WAS ONLY INTERESTED IN CHARLIE.

JACK DUCKWORTH

Window cleaner Jack readily hung up his leathers for a job behind the Rovers' bar. Jack was one of the pub's best customers and his delight at the prospect of spending all day with ale was apparent. His wife Vera had reservations about his new post, but she was won over by a regular wage packet. Jack is in his element surrounded by Newton & Ridley's bitter and barmaids.

Fancying himself as an ageing Casanova, Jack has found it hard to accept that women do not find him attractive. He lusted after Gloria Todd and sent her roses "from an admirer". She was pleased at first, but after five roses she felt unnerved by the fact that she didn't know who was sending them. Jack lured her to a "meeting" in a local pub before revealing himself as her admirer. Poor Jack was stunned by Gloria's revulsion on discovering that he had been lusting after her. He received the same reaction from Tina Fowler when he took her out. She agreed a date with Jack with the intention of having some fun at his expense. He spent most of his wages on her in an attempt to impress, but Tina gave him just a goodnight peck on the cheek, refusing his offer of "a quickie on the back seat of the car". When Vera found out about the evening she took cruel revenge – cutting up all of Jack's trousers.

In 1989, Jack walked out of the pub when Bet questioned him over money missing from the till. Bet discovered that Jack had been giving wrong change to the customers and grew concerned. She was relieved when Vera told her Jack wasn't "on the fiddle", just losing his eyesight. Jack returned to work with his National Health specs. To help his confidence, Bet and the rest of the staff assured him he hadn't lost any of his rugged sex appeal. If anything, Bet suggested, the glasses made him look like Clark Kent. Within the month the glasses had broken and from then on Jack has held them together with sticking-plaster.

CHARLIE BRACEWELL

Retired ventriloquist Charlie only worked at the Rovers for a month in January 1989. He was an old act from Alec Gilroy's theatrical agency whom Alec took on as barman because he was cheap. Charlie found Betty irresistible and deeply offended her by goosing her. Betty threatened to leave if Charlie stayed and Bet secured his removal by introducing him to landlady Stella Rigby. Stella found him charming and poached him from the Rovers – just as Bet had planned.

CLEANERS

In the early years, Annie Walker fought a losing battle with mop and bucket, trying to keep the floors, tables and bartops clean. Until 1962 she cleaned the pub herself and then, after taking on her first cleaner, often wondered how she'd ever coped without that indispensable person – her char.

MARTHA LONGHURST

A lifelong customer at The Rovers Return, Martha became the first paid cleaner in 1962 at the age of 66. Her cronies in the Snug, Ena Sharples and

ANNIE WALKER WAS FORCED TO WIELD A MOP UNTIL SHE FINALLY PERSUADED JACK TO EMPLOY A CLEANER.

Minnie Caldwell, thought she must have had "a slate loose" to work under Mrs "High and Mighty" Walker, but Martha needed the money to boost her pension. After a few weeks, she had won Annie's confidence and was accompanying her on shopping trips. Martha was called upon during her spare time to help Annie prepare for parties and special occasions. Martha spent her last day at the Rovers spring-cleaning, despite suffering pains all day. That night, in the Rovers' Snug, she suffered a fatal heart attack.

CLEANER MARTHA LONGHURST WAS ABLE TO SUPPLY HER CRONIES WITH ALL THE GOSSIP ABOUT THE WALKERS.

HILDA OGDEN

Hilda Ogden joined the Rovers' staff in July 1964, shortly after moving into the Street. Her daughter Irma was already working at the pub as barmaid and recommended Hilda as Martha's replacement. Annie was initially impressed by Hilda's thorough workmanship and was soon commenting on how indispensable Mrs Ogden was. Annie was soon to revise her opinion.

Hilda's aspirations to rise up from the ranks of cleaning led her to hand in her notice regularly. Annie was often in the happy position of thinking she had rid herself of nosy, interfering Hilda but her elation was always short-lived; finding that her new posts were never as easy as her work at the Rovers, Hilda always returned with her tail between her legs. Once, in 1974, Hilda applied for a caretaking job and asked Annie for a reference. Although keen for Hilda to be successful, so that she would be rid of the troublesome Mrs Ogden, Annie couldn't bring herself to praise her in glowing terms after suffering years of Hilda's erratic performance as a cleaner. The reference she gave was a masterpiece of ambiguity: "Since Mrs Ogden joined my staff her conduct has been all I have come to expect of her. Her spirit of co-operation is out of the ordinary. Her attendance and her application to work are entirely consistent with her other aptitudes.... Should Mrs Ogden be successful in obtaining another post I cannot say how sorry I shall be to lose her, but I can say in truth that Mrs Ogden will leave a gap at The Rovers Return which I am quite sure no one else will be able to fill."

Hilda worked in the Rovers for a total of 23 years. During that time she worked under all the Walkers and the Gilroys and had to suffer Bet's temperamental transition from barmaid to landlady.

ANNIE FOUGHT A 20-YEAR BATTLE WITH HILDA OGDEN, TRYING TO ENSURE SHE EXERCISED HER ELBOW RATHER THAN HER TONGUE.

Mr Ogden – Stan – was also to prove indispensable on the other side of the bar as he became the pub's best customer. In his twenty years in the Street, Stan drank his way into the record books and was acknowledged by the brewery as an expert on their beer.

Hilda's proudest day came in 1986 when, as the pub's longest-serving member of staff, she performed the opening ceremony at the new Rovers Return, refurbished after the fire. Tragically, the next year she was involved in a violent robbery and was forced to give up work as she couldn't bring herself to leave her house for fear of the outside world. When she eventually left the Street in December 1987 to become a housekeeper in Derbyshire, the residents gave her a rousing send-off in the Rovers.

AMY BURTON

Pensioner Amy replaced Hilda as cleaner at the Rovers in late 1987. She had moved to the Street to live with her daughter Vera Duckworth, and her son-in-law Jack had urged

JACK DUCKWORTH'S WORKING
CONDITIONS WERE WORSENED
BY THE ARRIVAL OF MOTHER-
IN-LAW AMY.

SANDRA STUBBS

Sandra turned up for her interview at the Rovers with a black eye. When questioned about it by Alec Gilroy, Sandra explained she had escaped a violent husband and was starting afresh with her 14-year-old son Jason. But Sandra's colleagues at the Rovers didn't quite believe her story once they met charming Ronnie Stubbs. Bet gave Ronnie Sandra's new address and was shocked when, a short time later, Jason rushed into the bar asking for help, as his father was beating his mother. Bet took charge of Jason whilst Sandra, bloody and battered, was taken to hospital for tests. The police persuaded Sandra to make an official complaint and obtain an exclusion order, freeing her from vicious Ronnie.

In November 1988, Sandra fought barmaid Gloria Todd when Gloria confessed she was having an affair with the new man in Sandra's life, Pete Shaw. A couple of months later

her to find a part-time job in order to get her out of the house. Jack was stunned to find her working at the Rovers where he worked as barman! Amy hastily resigned from the pub in March 1988 when Jack caught her stealing bottled beer from the shelves.

SANDRA STUBBS'
ATTEMPT TO FIND
HAPPINESS WAS
SHATTERED BY HER
FRIEND GLORIA
TODD.

Sandra resigned in order to spend more time with Jason, who was getting into trouble with the police.

When Sandra left The Rovers Return, landlord Alec Gilroy decided that it wasn't worth paying good money for a replacement when he already employed a bar full of women. Since then Bet and the barmaids have been forced to roll up their sleeves, don a pinny and clean the pub. When Alec left for Southampton, Bet discovered he had kept Hilda on the payroll and had been claiming tax deductions for her!

SIX OF THE BEST

THROUGHOUT THE 32-YEAR television history of *Coronation Street*, many of the stories have revolved around the Rovers, its staff and customers. Some – such as Fred Gee's outing in Annie's Rover, which ended in the lake – have been hilariously funny; others – such as the death of Jack Walker – have been tragic.

The pub has been seen in nearly every episode of the programme. Its set has appeared more often than any other, and within its walls many of the best storylines have been played out. Retold here are six of those stories, laid out in episodes as they originally appeared. Two are from the 1960s, two from the 1970s and two from the 1980s.

EPISODE 194

THE WALKERS' SILVER WEDDING

Written by EDDIE MAGUIRE AND ADELE ROSE
Transmitted 22 October 1962

"WELL IF THAT'S the sort of muck we're havin', I'm havin' me supper before I go." Turning up her nose at a tin of salmon in the corner shop, Ena Sharples was sceptical about that evening's private function at The Rovers Return.

To celebrate their silver wedding anniversary, Jack and Annie Walker were going to throw a party for all their friends and regulars. Annie was upset that neither of their children, Billy and Joan, would be present for the occasion, so Jack had thrown open the Rovers' doors to the regulars in an attempt to cheer her up. Rising to the occasion, and grasping the opportunity to show the commoners how to entertain in style, Annie had ordered the salmon along with olives and paté.

Whilst Ena turned her nose up at Annie's planned fare, Jack Walker had already had enough of his wife's catering. She had spent the entire day in her best apron, preparing the spread for the occasion. Jack, a man who preferred plain cooking, was not as tolerant as Annie would have wished: "I've been rushed off me feet in 'ere from first thing, an' every time I look for you yer 'idin' be'ind a stuffed olive." Annie refused to raise her voice in argument – it was after all their wedding anniversary: "You can't prepare a buffet for twenty or so people with a flick of the fingers. And I wouldn't mind, but anyone would think I wanted it, anyone would think I was making this party for my sake."

If Annie was preparing the party for her

JACK AND ANNIE HAD FIRST MET DURING THE DEPRESSION. HE HAD SPOTTED HER GAZING INTO A MURKY CANAL AND MISTAKENLY THOUGHT SHE WAS PLANNING TO THROW HERSELF IN. ANNIE WAS STUNNED WHEN THE YOUNG MAN HAD GRAPPLED WITH HER, REFUSING TO LET SUCH A BEAUTY KILL HERSELF.

guests' sakes, they were not aware. Most of them regarded the party as a chance for Mrs High-and-Mighty Walker to swank and show off her best cutlery, though they made every attempt to shine themselves.

At Miami Modes Department Store, Barker Street, Weatherfield, Mrs Elsie Tanner, divorcée, startled her colleague in the Slightly Better Dress Department by announcing she was going to wear her black outfit to the party. Her colleague and best friend, Dot Greenhalgh, was puzzled, knowing Elsie didn't own a black dress. "No, but she has" said Elsie with a twinkle in her eye, crossing the shop-floor to a dressed dummy. As Dot protested, Elsie unzipped the gown and slipped it off the dummy: "C'mon, Tallulah – my need is greater than thine."

When she walked into the Rovers' bar, Elsie was greeted by a mixed reaction. The men adored the dress: "Looks like she's been poured into it." In the Snug, Ena Sharples was more critical: "What can y'expect? Where there's no sense, there's no shame. She's only ter sneeze an' it'll be on't floor. It's far too tight for 'er – it'll stop 'er circulation."

As the guests arrived, Jack found it impossible to serve everyone on his own and so he interrupted Annie's preparations to tell her she was required behind the counter: "Oh, I couldn't possibly Jack, I've the paper serviettes to fold yet."

Jack finally snapped when his wife maintained he was just being tiresome; there was hardly anyone in the pub after all: "'Appen things 'ave livened up a bit since you put in yer last public appearance four hours ago – an I want some 'elp!"

Annie was upset by his manner; couldn't he see she was going to all this trouble because she didn't want to let him down? "Are you tryin' to pick a quarrel with me? Coming in here ordering me about. And on one of my happiest days, too."

Slowly the couple's voices rose until they were rowing together. Annie realised they were losing control of the situation and, blinking away the tears, caught Jack's attention. He put his arm around her: "Today of all days. We ought to be right ashamed of ourselves, the pair of us." Annie was in total agreement: "You see, love, we can't manage without each other."

As they embraced, thirsty customer Len Fairclough barged in waving his pint pot. He stopped dead when he saw the embrace and begged their pardon. Annie laughed: "Oh, it's quite alright. We are married you know".

As soon as the doors were closed to the general public, the party started to swing. With the record player on full volume, the music thumped, and so did Annie's head. With a false smile on her face, she swallowed aspirins and stuck to water whilst the guests attempted to drink the pub dry. Len Fairclough was in his element: "I dunno wharrit is about beer, burrit always tastes better on licensed premises after closin' time."

In the Snug, Ena and her friend Minnie Caldwell listened in as the ladies in the Public admired the presents the Walkers had received: "I don't know about this do costin' 'em a lot o' money, it looks as though they've made a profit on it."

Although usually interested only in hymns, Ena enjoyed the modern music playing on the

TEETOTAL LEONARD SWINDLEY FOUND HIMSELF GETTING LIGHT-HEADED DURING THE PARTY AS LEN FAIRCLOUGH HAD SPIKED HIS DRINKS WITH VODKA. ELSIE TANNER AND DOT GREENHALGH WERE AMUSED BY SWINDLEY'S UNCHARAC-TERISTIC BEHAVIOUR UNTIL HE DROPPED A TRIFLE OVER ELSIE'S BORROWED DRESS.

record player and joined in: "...There's a lovely moon outside." Her friend Minnie was puzzled: "Oh, no, it was cloudin' over as we come in."

In the Rovers' living room, the guests looked over Annie's buffet with curiosity. The sausages on sticks were the first seen in Coronation Street and no one could fathom what to do with the pickled walnuts. With a few drinks inside him, Jack started to relax: "I'm enjoyin' meself, now I'm gettin' in the mood. They say the first twenty years are the worst. If yer 'air's not grey by the time your silver weddin' comes along, gettin' ready for it'll take care o' that."

Annie, on the other hand, was not enjoying the party: "It's this headache, love. I've drugged myself with aspirin and it isn't doing a scrap of good." She announced her decision to go to bed and asked Jack to get rid of the guests: "Say goodnight for me love. I just couldn't face that Ya-Ya twist thing again."

Annie went upstairs and was surprised when Jack joined her a few minutes later. She was amazed when he explained that the guests were still enjoying themselves and he hadn't the heart to throw them out; besides, Len had promised to lock up after them.

Annie grew alarmed to hear the party getting rowdier. She was horrified as mysterious crashes sounded from downstairs: "My best sherry glasses! Gone to smithereens." Her

> ### William Roache (Ken Barlow) on Annie and Jack Walker's marriage:
>
> *" If ever there was a complementary relationship, it was Annie and Jack's. Annie had all the pretensions of grandeur, of being in charge and improving herself socially. She would often get out of line but all it needed from Jack was 'Ee, Annie!' and it put it all in perspective."*

voice travelled down to the guests as they stopped their revelries to listen to the row. Elsie was amused by Annie's dramatic screeches until lay-preacher Leonard Swindley tried to tempt her with the sherry trifle; the dish was too heavy for him and he dropped the trifle all over Elsie's dress. Dot stared in horror at the ruined gown as Elsie made a vain attempt to mop up the mess.

Upstairs in bed, Jack tried to shut Annie up but she was in no mood to be tolerant: "You're worn out – you're worn out! Who was it who made four dozen sausage rolls, eight dozen assorted fingers, three dozen..." She was interrupted mid-flow by the arrival of Len: "Would you mind keepin' yer voices down? We're tryin' to 'ave a party downstairs!"

Annie was not amused.

THE WALKERS WERE INDIGNANT WHEN LEN INTERRUPTED THEIR ROW IN THEIR OWN BEDROOM.

EPISODE 357

MARTHA'S DEATH

Written by JOHN PENNINGTON
Transmitted 13 May 1964

THE SIGHT OF CLEANER Martha Longhurst intently scrubbing the floor of the Public bar bemused landlady Annie Walker: "I must say you're very conscientious this morning, Mrs Longhurst. Is it because it's May?"

Martha, always suspecting Annie's speeches of having hidden meanings, was in no mood for general niceties: "I'm not workin' meself to death for me 'ealth, you know. I've got me purpose... Business, in town... Passport Office."

Martha had been invited to join her family on a holiday in Spain. For years her daughter Lily had treated her badly, getting in contact with her only when it suited. And it suited Lily to invite her mother to holiday with them; who else would be willing to look after the children all day whilst Lily stretched out in the sun? Martha, although fully aware of Lil's motives, convinced herself that a free holiday wasn't something to turn down: "I'm not gerrin' a crick in me neck strainin' up tryin' to see the sun from this 'ole, this year."

NEVER HAVING VENTURED FURTHER AFIELD THAN
BLACKPOOL, MARTHA WAS THRILLED WITH HER NEW PASS-
PORT. IF ONLY THE PAINS IN HER HEAD WOULD GO AWAY...

While Martha looked forward to her week in the sun, her neighbour Frank Barlow was yearning to leave the Street for a new life in Wilmslow. Frank had won on the Premium Bonds and had sold his thriving DIY shop to a supermarket chain. A life of luxury awaited him in Bramhall and he took every opportunity to remind the people he was leaving behind just what a dump Coronation Street was. Martha,

LEFT: FOR TWO YEARS 68-YEAR-OLD MARTHA SUPPLE-
MENTED HER PENSION BY CLEANING AT THE ROVERS.

like many of the residents, resented his new-found affluence: "You'll burst wi' business, you will, if yer not careful!"

Frank ignored her and told the Walkers of the "treat" he had in store: "I want to lay on summat special for me friends. I'm going to have a party here tonight after closing – a slap-up do for the whole street – pineapple on sticks, Tia Maria cocktails – money no object."

Martha decided to use the occasion of Frank's party to show off her first ever status symbol – her new passport. She dressed in her best coat and hat as she went calling on her life-long friend Ena Sharples. Ena was immedi-ately suspicious of Martha's outfit: "Why spring that on me? You wear that for weddin's, funer-als an' Sundays if you step outside; not includin' when yer on the fish."

Martha tried to ignore the swipe, smug in

the knowledge that she was going abroad – something Ena had not managed. Ena tried to show she wasn't bothered: "You're never goin' to see Spain, and even if you do, all you'll get is the inside of a hotel bedroom with two squalling kids round you."

Once in the Rovers, Martha was bothered by the fact that the Snug was full of strangers. Not only was there a man sitting in her chair but Ena's purse had not opened: "Nobody'll catch me buyin' booze when it's on free tap after the bell's gone."

As Jack Walker called time, flashing the house lights on and off, his wife Annie began to lay out the sandwiches and snacks she had hastily prepared. Concepta Hewitt helped her with the plates whilst Annie complained about Frank's attitude, of lording it over them all: "Of course, it was typical of Mr Barlow to just spring this on us right at the last moment. The whole thing, given a little more notice, could have been done a great deal better in the Select. We haven't the facilities. How I could be expected to make all these canapés on my own, I just don't know. And I notice Mrs Longhurst skived off quickly enough. She didn't offer to lend a hand, though she's sitting in there now, waiting to be first to the drinks."

Frank Barlow stuffed cigars in everyone's pockets, telling them all in a loud voice that the drinks were on him and the champagne would soon be flowing. He upset Annie by aggressively clearing the non-regulars out of the bar: "Stop him Jack. He's being most offensive. These people are our livelihood."

As soon as the offending stranger had vacated the seat in the Snug, Martha jumped into her usual chair. Ena thought she was acting irrationally, but Martha did not care: "This is my chair. I've always sat in it. It's become part of me."

Picking up the passport, Ena retorted: "You'd better take it to Spain wi' yer, 'ave it listed on yer passport under special peculiarities."

Ena was one of the first to the bar when Jack announced it was free drinks time: "I'm not suppin' stout. I'm suppin' gin, an' some o' that champagne stuff. It warms the cockles of the 'eart." She advised Martha to stick to sherry, it being Spanish wine.

The residents took advantage of the free drinks and totally ignored Frank, who pompously stood on a chair to deliver a speech about his own good fortune. He was unperturbed by the sea of backs he faced. Martha started flashing her passport around, and then Len Fairclough attempted to persuade Ena to give them "a touch of the Winifred Atwell's" on the piano. At first Ena refused: "I'll 'ave you know Len Fairclough I reserve my musical talents for songs of praise, not a bar-room orgy." But she was won round by the promise of a double champagne.

Whilst the guests gathered around the piano, laughing and drinking, Martha suddenly felt very alone. She became subdued and drew away from the crowd with her sherry and passport. Ena changed tunes from

---

Eileen Derbyshire (Emily Nugent) on filming "Martha's Death":

"Even at the filming, everybody was still having that outside hope that there would be a reprieve for Lynne Carol the actress and Martha the character. There was this terrible double bind of having to be singing and laughing whilst your throat was being constricted by the tears. There were tears in people's eyes and they were rolling down cheeks. It was a really horrible emotional experience."

WHILST HER FRIENDS AND
NEIGHBOURS ENJOYED A GOOD
SING-SONG, MARTHA SUF-
FERED A FATAL HEART ATTACK
IN THE ROVERS' SNUG.

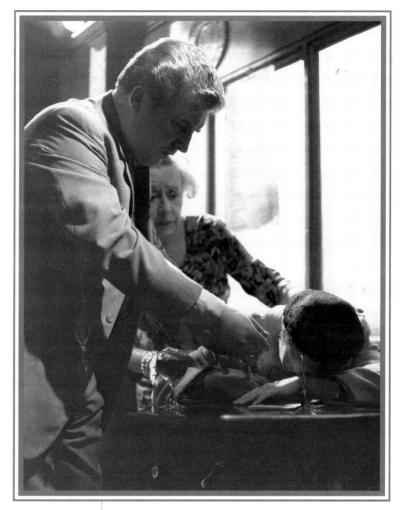

"Moonlight Bay" to "I'll be Your Valentine", as Martha sat quietly in her chair in the Snug. Annie, at the bar, watched through the open Snug doorway as Martha flicked through the blank pages in her passport. Suddenly Martha felt flushed and pulled open her top button. Pain shot through her head and body. Her hand shakily removed her glasses and placed them on the table top before knocking the hat off her head. She closed her eyes to escape the stab of pain shooting through her and slowly her body crumpled, her face falling forward onto her arms crossed on the table. She shuddered and then stopped breathing.

Myra Booth, singing at the piano with the other guests, laughed with her husband Jerry and pointed out Martha's figure, joking that she'd had too much sherry. Jerry alerted Jack to the fact Martha was drunk and the landlord went to investigate. What he found made his blood run cold. He rushed back into the Public to get Annie, who was followed by Len Fairclough. Len raised Martha's head and felt her pulse.

One by one the guests stopped singing and turned towards the open Snug door. Ena, with her back to the Snug, was the last to realise something was terribly wrong. She stopped playing the keys and slowly turned round in time to hear Len say words which struck her heart: "She's dead." Ena rose from the piano stool and, as the residents drew back, she stumbled into the Snug, the frosted glass door slowly closing after her.

The party ended abruptly; the guests left in ones and twos until only the Walkers, Ena and the late Martha Longhurst remained in the pub.

That night, for the first time in *Coronation Street*'s four-year history, the credits rolled in silence. The usual film sequence of rooftops was replaced by a single shot of a table top. On the table were three objects – a glass of sherry, a pair of spectacles and a passport.

EPISODE 1749

ANNIE'S ANNIVERSARY

Written by JOHN STEVENSON
Transmitted 19 October 1977

*J*ACK AND ANNIE WALKER had taken over the tenancy of The Rovers Return in late October 1937. Jack had died in 1970, but Annie had remained in the pub. In 1977, barmaid Bet Lynch discovered that Annie would soon be celebrating her 40th anniversary at the pub, and decided to mark the occasion. Without Annie's knowledge, Bet and Betty Turpin planned an evening Annie would never forget.

As the day arrived, Betty started to wonder why they were going to all the trouble, as Annie, making no allowances for the day, was her usual self: "We must be stark staring mad. She tears strips off us as though we were old wallpaper hanging on a damp wall – and here we are trying to organise a surprise party for her. I'm wondering why we bother."

Cleaner Hilda Ogden was upset to discover that the party had been planned behind her back: "It wouldn't have got all over the place from me. I can keep a confidence you know. I could have helped you plan things."

Both Betty and Hilda were curious as to what Bet's special surprise was going to be, but she wasn't letting on.

The regulars were keen to help spring the party but were mystified as to how Bet was going to achieve the impossible. As Ken Barlow put it: "How are you managing to organise a party for Annie Walker in her own pub without her finding out?"

Bet had an answer to the question. The food was stored at the Langtons' at No. 5, pianist Ernie Bishop moved the piano into the Public from the Select, while Betty's main task was keeping unsuspecting Annie in her living room. The party guests filled the pub and Betty asked Annie to help out in the bar. As she walked

JACK HAD BEEN TAKEN FROM ANNIE AFTER 33 YEARS OF MARRIAGE. THERE WOULD NEVER BE ANOTHER MAN IN HER LIFE.

into the Public, the regulars cheered and raised their glasses.

Annie was genuinely moved with emotion at seeing the obvious regard the regulars held for her. She choked back a tear as they sang "For She's A Jolly Good Fellow" but Bet was puzzled by something: "Mrs Walker, do you mind telling me something? You've got your best frock on. You only ever put that on for very special occasions..."

Annie smiled: "That's true dear, and I think I see what you're suspecting. Shall I just say that after 40 years in these premises there is nothing – absolutely nothing – that altogether escapes my notice?"

Bet was amazed by her employer, but delighted in telling her there was one surprise she didn't know about. She flung open the pub doors and Billy Walker strolled in, to his mother's immense delight.

As the party picked up momentum, Annie mingled with her regulars. Elsie Tanner tried to make the most of the situation, commenting that 40 years was a long time and didn't it make Annie feel her age? Annie's reply was sweet: "But you must remember, I started very young. Yes, when Jack and I took this place I was barely old enough to set foot in licensed premises – let alone to run one."

Alone with Billy, Annie couldn't help but think about Jack. She missed him so much and her love for him was undiminished. "I can't help wondering where 40 years have gone to. It seems like no time at all. They've been happy years for me, Billy – not all of them, but I know I've been a very fortunate woman. With your father, of course. And with my children." In one of their closest moments, Annie squeezed her son's hand.

The highlight of the evening was the arrival of brewery executive Richard Cresswell. He was related to the brewery

> ### Betty Driver on Annie Walker:
> *"Bet and Betty always tried to get one up on Annie behind her back, but they never quite managed it."*

family and his father Douglas was one of Annie's oldest friends. Richard was full of admiration for the landlady: "I think this party here tonight, this, as it were, spontaneous tribute, tells us something very important of how Mrs Walker's customers feel about her. At Newton & Ridley we too feel very strongly about Mrs Walker. For 40 years The Rovers Return has been a byword for those qualities which we most value in a public house – courtesy, friendliness, and, of course, a certain very individual style, the seasoning which gives all these other qualities their finest flavour." With that, he presented a glowing Annie with a silver tray engraved by the brewery.

The party continued well into the night as Annie and her guests enjoyed Mr Cresswell's offer of free drinks. Ernie Bishop on the piano struck up "We've Been Together Now For Forty Years" and everyone toasted Annie – Queen of the Rovers.

BREWERY BOSS RICHARD CRESSWELL PRESENTED ANNIE WITH AN ENGRAVED TRAY TO MARK HER LONG ASSOCIATION WITH THE COMPANY.

EPISODE 1893

LORRY CRASHES INTO THE PUB

Written by LES DUXBURY
Transmitted 12 March 1979

DEIRDRE LANGTON, recently separated from her husband Ray, had called at the Rovers to return a knitting pattern to Annie Walker. Knowing Annie's disapproval of children on licensed premises, Deirdre left her two-year-old daughter Tracy outside the pub in her pushchair.

She had only been in Annie's back room a couple of minutes when the pub was shaken by a terrible crash. Annie froze, but Deirdre rushed through the hall into the bar. The scene was chaotic, with dust and smoke everywhere. Deirdre pushed past barmaids Betty Turpin and Bet Lynch, who were helping each other up off the floor where they had been thrown. On the other side of the bar, the lunch-time

customers were sprawled over the furniture and floor. There was glass and timber everywhere, but Deirdre rushed past the debris and pulled open the pub door. There, just where she'd left Tracy, was a four-foot pile of timber, thrown into the front of the pub by an overturned lorry which lay across the street. Deirdre began to pull frantically at the wood, screaming her daughter's name.

Deirdre's neighbours Hilda Ogden and Rita Fairclough were next on the scene. The noise of the crash sent them hurrying out of their homes to investigate. The machinists at Baldwin's Casuals streamed out of the loading-bay, while social worker Ken Barlow pulled on his jacket as he sprinted across the street from the Community Centre. Summing up the situation as he saw it, he took immediate control. Remaining calm as Deirdre screamed hysterically, he issued instructions: "Right, the first thing we want is the police, don't we... Rita, phone them."

As Rita rushed to her phone, Ken crouched down to see how badly the lorry's driver was hurt, as the cab was now resting on the cobbles.

Inside the pub, the shocked customers started to stir. Factory boss Mike Baldwin found himself lying on the floor, his suit ripped and torn. His leg, trapped under a cast-iron table, sent waves of pain tearing through his body. Len Fairclough, who moments before had been sitting drinking with his old friend

> ### Anne Kirkbride (Deirdre Langton) on filming the lorry crash:
> *"I spent two days shouting 'Tracy', stood on a wood pile with smoke being pumped out. It was easy to do because the whole thing was so horrifically real. It was easy to be traumatised in that situation and to actually feel that you were desperately searching, that under all that wood was a little girl."*

Alf Roberts, knew instantly that his own arm had been broken. With his other arm he tried to pull away the timber that half covered Alf, who lay motionless, sprawled on the floor. Bet Lynch had no broken bones and she quickly joined Len to help uncover Alf from under the pile of wood. Her colleague Betty Turpin tired to stop the blood gushing from a wound on her arm where she had been sliced by flying glass. Annie Walker, taking in the scene, swooned against the bar flap, unable to speak from shock. It was then that Bet heard Deirdre's screams and told Betty to find out what was going on outside.

Betty found Deirdre trying desperately to pull the timber away from the door: "Tracy's outside! I left Tracy out here!".

Rita returned, running across the cobbles as fast as her high-heeled boots would allow her. With her came shopkeeper Renee Roberts. Having established that the lorry driver was now dead, Ken left him and climbed over the timber towards Deirdre, trying to reassure her: "It's alright Deirdre, help's coming". He began to help her pull the timber away but the pile never seemed to end.

Hearing sirens approaching, Bet advised Len not to move Alf in case his back was injured. Len refused to leave his friend's side and tried to encourage him: "It's alright mate, we'll have you out of here in no time, no danger". Annie did not help matters when she became hysterical at the sight: "Poor Alf... he's dead isn't he! He looks dead!" Bet shouted at her and calmed her, leading her into the back room so she could sit down.

The police arrived in force and started to

AS KEN BARLOW HELPED DEIRDRE OVER THE TIMBER, NEITHER OF THEM COULD HAVE GUESSED THAT TWO YEARS LATER THEY WOULD BE MAN AND WIFE.

help with the timber. Police Sergeant Broady took charge of the situation. His most pressing concern was Tracy's fate. A clearing was made in the wood and Broady and Ken led Deirdre over the timber to safety. At first she refused to leave the pub: "Where is she? Where's Tracy? Why haven't you got her out? Tracy, it's Mummy!" Deirdre started to tear at the timber again and had to be restrained by Broady. He led her firmly onto the street where her friend Emily Bishop ushered her into her house. For the first time, Deirdre started to cry.

Hearing that there were injured people in the pub, Broady realised he needed more men and issued orders: "Watch things out here. Don't let anybody go near. And put Control in the picture. Tell 'em we need more bodies. It's a major incident."

Realising that their husbands were in the pub, Rita and Renee dodged the policemen and scrambled up the timber behind Broady, following him into the shattered bar. Broady evacuated the unhurt customers from the pub as the ambulance men arrived. Renee became hysterical at the sight of her unconscious husband. Bet tended to Mike, though he complained when she offered him a glass of water and nothing stronger: "It's me flamin' leg that's injured, not me throat!"

The crowd outside the Rovers was growing. Bystanders joined the police and fire brigade in removing the timber. Everyone's mind was on the little girl trapped beneath the wood. The Fire Chief called for silence but nothing could be heard from under the timber. Broady braced himself to tell Deirdre her baby was probably dead.

Sitting in Emily's parlour, Deirdre, ashen with shock, refused to remain hidden away from the search and attempted to leave, but pensioner Ena Sharples stopped her: "Of course Tracy wants you. But they have to find her first. And they're looking hard, very hard. Now sit down and we'll come and tell you when she's found. And she's going to be found, make no mistake about that."

Covered with a red blanket, Alf was carried out the back of the pub on a stretcher. Len, his arm in a splint, made a promise to himself as he was led to the ambulance: "I'm going to give up going to pubs after this." His wife knew him better: "That'll be the day!"

In the Rovers' living room, Betty tried to establish some normality by making tea for Annie, who was haunted by the noise of the sirens: "The gates of Hell will sound like that, when they swing open to receive us all. Has the world gone mad? Why do these things happen? What is the point? Why all this senseless, stupid destruction of life and property? What is the point of beginning anything, anything at all, if eventually you're going to destroy it?"

Once the pub had been cleared of customers, Bet allowed her calm facade to drop. She crumpled into tears at the thought of Tracy buried under the rubble. Rita led her to the back and poured her a brandy: "I'm sorry Rita. I hardly ever cry. You can't afford to, can you, when you've got this much eye-liner and mascara on."

A fireman crawled under the timber and retrieved a battered doll. By this time Deirdre had convinced herself that Tracy was dead: "It's all my fault. First there were me and Ray. I sent him away. Now she's gone... It's my fault. I started it. Families have to stick together. That's what you have a family for. They're like flowers. Take one petal away and before you know it, it's all gone. Tracy's dead. Like me and Ray. Her family's dead, so she's dead. It follows. Logical. How am I going to tell Ray? He adored her."

Emily felt helpless as Deirdre dissolved into tears, but Ena, with years of heartbreak and human suffering behind her, knew that Deirdre had to cry. Ena offered comfort in the only way she knew how, offering up a prayer to God: "Dear Lord, we pray you look down with love and compassion on this child in her hour of need. Help her to be strong, and patient. And not to be afraid. We ask this in the name of thy dear son, Jesus Christ."

The residents tried to get things back to normal. As Bet and Betty cleaned up inside the pub, Bet found Alf's silver fountain pen amongst the rubble and marvelled that it didn't have a scratch on it. With Tracy's fate still uncertain, Bet sank despondently into a chair, telling Betty she'd had enough: "I just need to let go for a minute, that's all. Oh, I'll soon snap back into action. You can depend on that, can't you? Good old Bet, always manages to keep a stiff upper lip. Keeps the smile pasted on. It's not always easy you know Betty, not even for me!"

RITA,
RENEE AND HILDA LOOK ON AS
RESCUE WORKERS TRY TO FREE TRACY AND GET HELP
TO THE DRINKERS IN THE ROVERS.

In a rare insight into their relationship, Bet let the mask slip and revealed her true, vulnerable feelings. Betty responded out of love: "I'll tell you something, luvvie. There's lots of times when I'm ever so grateful to you for it; I get up in the mornings to an empty house, and there's not much point to anything. And then I come to work and I think, 'Bet'll make me smile', and you do duck."

Keeping an eye on Renee's shop, Vera Duckworth caught a youth taking advantage of the opportunity to help himself to the cigarettes. She let him go after belting him around the head.

The stillness at No. 3 was shattered by Broady banging on the front door. As Ena and Emily went to answer it, Deirdre covered her ears, trying to shut out the expected news of Tracy's death.

At the door, Broady broke the news to Emily and Ena that after a thorough search, Tracy had not been found – she was not under the timber at all. Delighted, Emily rushed back to tell Deirdre that Tracy was safe, only to find the parlour deserted and the back door open. Fearing the worst, Deirdre had disappeared.

The credits rolled over the image of Deirdre wandering down an alleyway clutching a toy elephant.

The story of the Rovers' crash was wrapped up in the next episode, when Tracy was found in the company of a mentally disturbed young woman who had snatched the baby moments before the lorry crashed into the pub. Deirdre was found standing over the canal in a trance. She only came away from danger when Emily rushed Tracy to the scene, and mother and daughter were reunited.

For Alf Roberts, the scars of the crash took longer to heal. He was in a coma for three weeks and suffered a personality change when he eventually came round.

EPISODE 2631

⚬ FIRE AT THE ROVERS ⚬

Written by H. V. KERSHAW
Transmitted 18 June 1986

*I*T HAD STARTED the night before. Landlady Bet Lynch had employed local pianist Julian Marshall to entertain in the Public, but most people's attention was drawn by the arrival of Alan Bradley, who had been barred the previous night for thumping trouble-maker Terry Duckworth. Bet used her discretion to allow both Terry and Alan back into the pub once she had established that no one was going to be used as a punch-bag.

Throughout the day, the electric pumps and kitchen appliances had been stopping as the fuses kept blowing in the fuse-box, located in the cellar. The whole system was antiquated and cellarman Jack Duckworth realised there was little he could do, long-term, to repair the box, other than keep replacing the fuses. Bet, however, had complete trust in his abilities: "Worry not, booze artists. Cometh the hour, cometh the man with the power an' the knowledge! Superspark'll soon have the ale flowin'."

By 10pm the customers were getting fractious as the lights kept going out, but Julian came up trumps for Bet by keeping spirits high and the residents soon settled down to a night of singing around the piano in candlelight. It was almost disappointing when Jack

THE RESIDENTS OF CORONATION STREET WORKED AS ONE IN A BID TO RESCUE BET FROM THE INFERNO.

brought forth light again. Jack was enjoying his moment of glory and Bet's praise for his electrical prowess, and so, faced with the knowledge that the 5-amp fuses would keep blowing, he substituted a 30-amp one.

After the regulars and staff had gone home, Bet decided to leave the clearing-up until the morning. She took a paperback to bed in her pink boudoir, full of satin cushions and lacy frills. She finally got to sleep a little after one o'clock, unaware that down in the cellar the overloaded consumer unit had started to smoke. Soon the tinder-dry cables behind the mounting-board were ignited by the high-resistance connection and the fuse box burst into flames.

At 5am the action really started. Kevin Webster, the lodger at No. 13 Coronation Street, was returning from an all-night concert in Sheffield with his girlfriend Sally Seddon. Kevin was tired after eight hours of rock and roll and refused Sally's attempts to stop him from going home without more than a good-night kiss. She snatched his house keys and dashed off down the street; he caught up with her opposite the Rovers and playfully struggled with her for the key. It was then that Sally's face registered horror as she saw smoke billowing from under the Rovers' door. With Kevin asking her what was wrong, she uttered just one word: "Fire!".

Suddenly the Street sprang to life. Kevin hammered at the Rovers' door, calling for Bet to wake up, while Sally screamed for the Barlows at No. 1 to stir themselves and call the fire brigade. Percy Sugden, caretaker at the Community Centre, was roused by the commotion and came to investigate. When he saw the smoke he told Kevin to follow him to the Centre where he had a ladder that could be used to reach Bet.

Still in his dressing-gown, Ken Barlow organised the evacuation of his household as Kevin told him how bad the fire was: "Get Deirdre an' the kid out! It could spread." Ken rushed into the street calling to his wife, "Get Tracy out!", and Deirdre was thrown into a panic as the smoke began to reach their house. Clutching her nine-year-old daughter and the insurance policies wrapped in a towel, Deirdre followed him onto the street.

Meanwhile, Sally was making her way down the street, screaming for all she was worth for the residents to stir themselves. At No. 13, Hilda Ogden hurriedly took in her milk bottles; she later said it was a reflex action. Terry Duckworth threw himself into the scene, wearing nothing but track-suit bottoms. His army training came into use as he ordered the residents around, getting cars moved away from the Street and organising wet towels in case they were needed.

By this time, upstairs in her smoke-filled bedroom, Bet Lynch was finally woken up by the commotion outside her window. Rather than go to the window for help, she rushed to her door and attempted to escape through the pub itself. Her eyes blinded by the thick, stinging smoke, she crawled on her hands and knees towards the stairwell. When she finally got there, she hauled herself up on the banister to find the escape route cut off by roaring flames, which licked and crackled up the stairs towards her. She let out a heart-rending scream that echoed around the pub, startling her neighbours outside. Somehow she managed to work her way back to her bedroom, banging the door shut behind her as she fell to her knees and vomited up the smoke that had congealed in her stomach. She cried out for help but her creaky voice was hardly more than a whisper.

Outside in the daylight,

> ### Sally Whitaker (Sally Seddon) on filming the Rovers' fire:
> *"It was just the most exciting thing that had ever happened. This wonderful building that everyone in the country knew was about to burn down."*

BY THE TIME THE FIRE BRIGADE ARRIVED, THE FIRE AT THE ROVERS HAD TAKEN HOLD AND KEVIN HAD ALREADY BROKEN INTO THE PUB TO SAVE BET.

Kevin climbed the ladder and stood on the top of the pub sign. Wrapping Ivy Tilsley's wet towel around his face, he peered into the window. He smashed the window with a brick just as a fire engine turned the street corner by the shop. The residents urged Kevin to come back and leave it to the fire brigade to rescue Bet, but Kevin, shouting that he could see her, climbed through the bedroom window. At that moment, the ground-floor window blew out, showering glass into the street and allowing the flames to leap out towards the rescuers. The residents ran screaming for safety.

Terry, worried for Kevin's safety, urged the firemen to hurry as they seemed to take an age, sorting equipment and clothing. The firemen, equipped with breathing apparatus, sprinted up their ladder and climbed into the bedroom to see Kevin, spluttering with the smoke, trying to drag unconscious Bet to safety. The professionals made him drop Bet and forced him out of the window to safety. Once out of the pub, an ambulance crew tried to take him to hospital for treatment but Kevin refused, maintaining there was nothing wrong with him. Sally and Hilda led the hero home as the residents cheered him.

Vera Duckworth tried to make light of the situation and was puzzled by her husband's unusual solemnness: "What's up with you? Frightened o' crackin' your face?" But Jack was realising that his trick with the fuse box had probably caused the fire.

The sight of Bet, her white nightgown grimy from smoke, being carried down the ladder over a fireman's shoulder drew the residents towards the Rovers, where the fire was by now well under control. As Bet's limp body

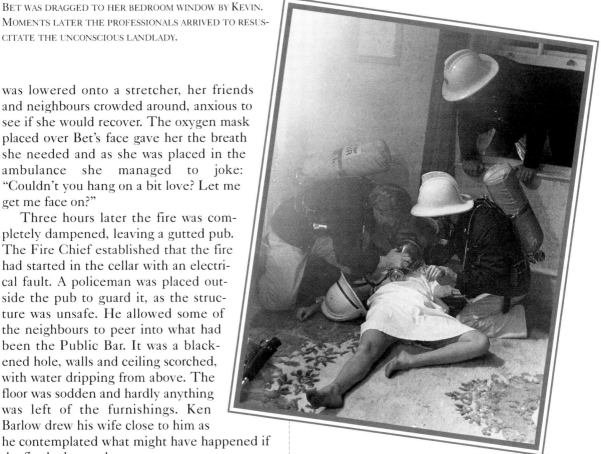

was lowered onto a stretcher, her friends and neighbours crowded around, anxious to see if she would recover. The oxygen mask placed over Bet's face gave her the breath she needed and as she was placed in the ambulance she managed to joke: "Couldn't you hang on a bit love? Let me get me face on?"

Three hours later the fire was completely dampened, leaving a gutted pub. The Fire Chief established that the fire had started in the cellar with an electrical fault. A policeman was placed outside the pub to guard it, as the structure was unsafe. He allowed some of the neighbours to peer into what had been the Public Bar. It was a blackened hole, walls and ceiling scorched, with water dripping from above. The floor was sodden and hardly anything was left of the furnishings. Ken Barlow drew his wife close to him as he contemplated what might have happened if the fire had spread.

After being questioned by the Fire Chief, worried Jack was left to confess to his son Terry that he had put "too hefty a fuse" in. The firemen seemed satisfied that the antiquated electrical wiring at the pub had been at fault, but Jack feared a brewery investigation. Later in the day he met with barmaids Betty Turpin and Gloria Todd. Betty had been to the brewery to see what their initial reaction was: "Saw a nice young fellah. One o' the Ridleys. Just gone on the board. He said they'd had this emergency meetin', they'd been round to the Rovers, inspected it, an' it'd be cheaper to pull it down."

The next day, after discharging herself from hospital, Bet met with the brewery bosses. Fully aware of Jack's bumbling attempts at electrical engineering, she decided to take the blame for the fire on herself. She came back to the Street to tell relieved Jack that the brewery were not after scapegoats, had admitted that the wiring had needed to be updated, and had had a change of heart over the pub's future. The Rovers was to be completely renovated.

A postscript to the story of The Rovers' fire is that when the pub was finished, Bet agreed to take Jack back on as potman. She did, however, give him one condition of employment: "I've pinned up a little card next to the phone. Number on it's an electrician. If a fuse ever blows, that's who you ring. We've got this place; let's try and hang on to it."

EPISODE 1759

BET MARRIES ALEC

Written by LES DUXBURY
Transmitted 9 September 1987

THE UNLIKELY UNION of mean, shifty Alec Gilroy and Bet Lynch, the original tart with a heart, stunned many of the regulars at The Rovers Return.

Bet had accepted Alec's proposal in the sun of Torremolinos. He had tracked her down there when she ran away because the repayments on the pub tenancy had became too much to cope with. Bet had resigned herself to serving as a barmaid for the rest of her life, having blown her one chance to run her own pub.

Alec had been given the tenancy of the pub in Bet's absence, and now he offered her a way to return to the Rovers with her head held high and be Queen of the pub – by returning as the landlord's wife. Bet was intrigued by his offer, but noticed that he had not mentioned love. When she questioned him about this he replied that he wasn't one to show his feelings and hadn't even told his mother that he loved her.

Back in Coronation Street, many people were surprised by the engagement as the pair seemed so incompatible, but Bet's mind was made up: "E's bin brought up in same school of life as what I 'ave. The tough one. Makes us birds of a feather. So maybe it's a marriage made in 'eaven."

Bet spent the night before her wedding at Gloria Todd's flat in Ashdale Road. Barmaid Gloria was to be Bet's bridesmaid and had done all she could to dissuade Bet from marrying Alec, whom she did not trust. However, on the morning of the wedding Gloria woke at 8am to find Bet laying out the grapefruit halves singing "There was I, waiting at the Church".

She refused to be pampered by Gloria or anyone else: "The last beauty sleep I had was in me cot. And even then only me mother thought it weren't a waste of time."

Gloria resisted Bet's attempt to control every minute of the day: "I've got this morning all mapped out. Breakfast. Then a long soak in a vanilla bubble bath. Then the hairdressers. And last but not least we bung you in your trousseau." Bet wasn't keen: "You mek me sound like a poodle bein' got ready for Crufts."

Alec had had a rougher night, reminiscing about his days as a bachelor with his best man Charles Halliday, a confirmed misogynist. The Rovers' cleaner, Hilda Ogden, found Alec flaked out in the living room in his nightwear. "Here comes the groom, face like a tomb" she warbled. She shook Alec awake and he explained he had spent most of the night awake after a frightening dream: "I was being chased through a bed of nettles. By a woman brandishing a red-hot poker."

Throughout the morning, Bet suffered pangs of doubt. After 47 years as a single girl, was she doing the right thing? "Who needs a husband? I mean, look at you, Glo. A nice little flat. A job you like. The odd date. I could still have all them. So what am I gettin' wed for? I keep thinking about me and Alec. When we're 64. What we'll be like then."

RESPLENDENT IN IVORY - BET'S WEDDING DRESS IS ON PERMANENT DISPLAY AT GRANADA STUDIO TOURS.

Gloria tried to reassure her: "You'll have a mink coat. And he'll probably be a Mason. If he's not one already. And you'll do a lot of cruising."

Alec, now in his suit and struggling with his carnation buttonhole, was attended to by cellarman Jack Duckworth. Like many of the men in the Street, Jack had had a fling with Bet in her barmaid days. Alec was unaware of this but grew suspicious when Jack cheerfully advised him to impregnate Bet as soon as possible as he'd be guaranteed peace and quiet if she was cooing over a baby: "Best years of my married life, when our Terry were a baby; Vera had her hands full. Hadn't time to mek me life miserable. So get Bet's name down for the puddin' club, boss.

Julie Goodyear (Bet Lynch) on filming Bet and Alec's wedding:
"My lasting memory of the wedding was arriving at the church to film, and literally hundreds of people had camped outside overnight. They were waiting for me to arrive, and in one voice they were chanting, 'Don't do it, don't do it'."

And between you and me, you won't exactly have to bend her arm in that direction." Alec stared coldly back at Jack's lecherous wink.

Betty Turpin attended Bet at Gloria's flat. She shared Gloria's contempt for Alec: "I know she's old enough to know what she's doing. But some women never are, are they, when it comes to chaps. We could save her from herself. Lock her in the bedroom. Drug her. Hit her over the head with something."

At that point, Bet floated into the room in her full-length ivory gown. Betty admired the dress while Gloria answered the ringing phone, assuring Alec everything was alright. Bet was amused to hear Alec was worried: "Should we give him a right fright and turn up quarter of an hour late?"

In the event, Bet was only seven minutes late and Alec was relieved when she finally walked down the aisle on Alf Roberts' arm, stepping in time to Purcell's famous strains. Bet was puzzled when Alec greeted her at the altar with a question: "How well do you know Jack Duckworth?"

ALL OF BET'S FRIENDS BELIEVED THE UNLIKELY MATCH WITH ALEC HAD NO FUTURE, ALTHOUGH THEY WISHED HER EVERY HAPPINESS.

Back in the Rovers, the offending cellarman was running the pub while everyone else was at the wedding. His flagging morale rose considerably when he was joined by glamorous Di, the catering organiser. He willingly left his pumps to "give her a hand" with the food.

Meanwhile, at St Mary's Parish Church, the Reverend Rawlinson declared the Gilroys man and wife after they had exchanged vows and rings. Alec was uncertain what to do at this point, as he had followed the vicar for his cues so far. Bet took the lead: "Well, go on, kiss me."

He did. As the couple and witnesses went to sign the register, the guests, all on Bet's side of the church, were united in their opinion of the ceremony. As the organist started up, Hilda Ogden turned to Betty with a question: "What's this they're playing?" "Oh, Perfect Love" was Betty's answer. Next to her in the pew, Rita Fairclough caught her eye. "Did you say something?" asked Betty. "Never said a word" was Rita's reply. Her face, however, matched Betty and Hilda's, showing nothing but doubt about the likely success of the union.

Outside the church, posing for photographs, Rita changed her mind slightly: "Hey, Hilda, they look better together than I thought they would." Hilda agreed: "Yeah, but I think he'd have been better off wearing them cube heels though. For the photographs."

The wedding party returned to the Rovers for the reception, laid out in the living room by the capable Di and the not-so-capable Jack. Jack was put out when Alec introduced him to Di's husband – his best man, Charles. Charles' speech offended the women with his low regard of marriage. Alec echoed Charles' speech, saying he too was surprised that he was now married. But then, becoming serious, he moved Bet by expressing his love for her: "But it's a very nice surprise. And it's one I've been looking forward to since the first day I met Bet. What more can a middle-aged chap with fat hairy legs say?"

After the speeches, Rita had a word for her old pal Bet: "Has anyone ever told you about the facts of life?"

"I was told about them sat on Co-op steps when I was twelve" was Bet's reply.

Alec stood watching Bet chatting to her pals and for the first time in their relationship, he had no doubts about the future. She caught his eye and raised a glass of champagne, and he was one happy little man: "I've done very well for meself today. Very well."

GLORIA TODD AND CHARLES HALLIDAY JOINED THE BRIDE AND GROOM OUTSIDE THE CHURCH, ALTHOUGH BOTH HAD TRIED TO STOP THE UNION.

HOW THEY BURNT DOWN
THE ROVERS

"For a moment it was real life and fantasy crossing over, because the Rovers actually had been destroyed. That set, which we knew so well and had done all that work in, was completely gone."

ANNE KIRKBRIDE

THE NATIONAL PRESS announced that the burning down on The Rovers Return was a direct ploy by the Granada bosses to beat EastEnders in the television ratings. This theory was laughable to the small band of people who were planning the fire. The whole story had been created, not to boost viewing figures, but to give the designer a chance to give the Rovers set a much-needed facelift. By the Spring of 1986, the set of The Rovers Return had been in existence for 26 years. The wallpaper had, of course, been changed during that time, and the paintwork touched up, but the general effect was that of a worn-out, shabby interior.

At this stage – years before Coronation Street would be given its own production centre and permanent sets – each set was erected in the studio every Wednesday for recording that week, and removed at the weekend so the studio could be dressed for another show. All this shifting of sets caused a lot of wear and tear.

The dressing of the Rovers set took longer than any other set because of its size and the number of props involved. Roy Graham, the series' designer, worried about the state of the flats that made up each section of the pub; on-screen they were looking very battered and the wallpaper in the Rovers was, by now, no longer obtainable. He brought this problem to the producer, John Temple, and the storyliners of the time, Tom Elliott and Paul Abbott (both are now writers on the programme).

Tom Elliott recalls: "We were asked if we could write some episodes without the Rovers, to give the designer the chance to update the interior. Both Paul and I felt it would be difficult to write episodes without The Rovers Return because that was where everyone met. However, the flats were in a bad state of repair and something drastic had to be done. We took the problem to the story conference with the idea that the pub could be damaged by fire; this would mean it would have to close and could be refurbished." The writers agreed that the fire would prove to be one of the most dramatic stories in the history of Coronation Street.

MEDICAL CREWS WERE ON HAND TO ENSURE THAT JULIE GOODYEAR WAS IN NO DANGER DURING THE FILMING OF THE FIRE.

When the scripts were written, Gareth Morgan, the director, was given the immense task of planning the episodes about the fire. As well as involving such a dramatic storyline, these episodes were to be the first in which every scene would be recorded on tape. Prior to this, all exterior scenes had been recorded on film whilst the studio scenes were on tape. The difference in quality between the two was very apparent and it was decided that the new process would be tested out for this dramatic story. The last major technical change in *Coronation Street* – that of changing from black and white to colour – had also occurred during a major disaster story, when a coach, with all the residents on board, crashed into a tree.

The scripts called for a fire to start in the Rovers' cellar, spread to the pub and eventually set the upstairs alight. Gareth Morgan picks up the story: "The only way we could reasonably do it was to use two sites: one was the existing Coronation Street lot, which we could use to blow out the windows and give the impression of fire inside and upstairs; and for the other we had to find an existing building in which we could reconstruct the Rovers, with its own basement where the fire could start, and then that building would be literally gutted. Which is what we did with The Pineapple Pub." The Pineapple was an old, disused pub on Water Street, at the back of Granada Studios. It was used occasionally by the company for location work and had last been used for *Coronation Street* in January 1984, as the pub where Bill Gregory took his long-lost love Elsie Tanner before they emigrated together. The studio owned the pub – the site is now part of the Granada Tours car-park – and the designers dressed the interior to match the Rovers down to the last detail.

The sequence of scenes shot on the Rovers' exterior lot took two Saturdays to complete. It was a very long shoot for all involved. The entire cast was involved in those episodes, along with more crew members than usually used, pyrotechnic experts to keep charge of the

fire, fire-tenders and medical crews. Everyone was aware that they were dealing with real fire and the situation could easily get out of control. However, no one was prepared for the intensity of the fire once it took hold.

The filming at The Pineapple was equally intense: the heat and gas explosions blew a cameraman out of a window. Gareth recalls: "People almost came to grief. This wasn't for lack of care, but in stories like this you cannot calculate what the effect is going to be."

Most of the cast were called in for the scenes to be shot on the Coronation Street lot, which opened with Kevin and Sally returning from a concert, and spotting the smoke coming from the pub. At the time, Sally Whittaker had played Sally Seddon for only five months. She still recalls the day of filming with awe: "I hadn't been in *Coronation Street* for very long and I still felt like a newcomer. There were lots of fire engines and ambulances and loads of people milling around that day and it was just the most exciting thing that had ever happened."

However, the excitement was replaced by nerves as the recording started and Sally had to spring into action: "My character had to spot the fire and then run down the street and knock on every door to wake everybody up. I remember knocking on the first door and I couldn't remember who lived at which house. So I had to be told as I went to each house."

Filming with Sally was actor Michael Le Vell, whose character, Kevin Webster, was to be the hero of the day, saving Bet from the flames. Like Sally, he felt honoured that his character was involved in such an important story: "I mean, The Rovers Return isn't just part of *Coronation Street*, it's an institution in itself. I felt flattered that my character helped save it. Gareth Morgan had us climbing up ladders and doing our own stunts and it actually felt that you were involved in a real fire situation."

As Sally and Kevin tried to wake up the rest of Coronation Street and rescue Bet from the pub, the residents appeared, one by one, to

flee the flames. For Anne Kirkbride – Deirdre Barlow – the situation was too real: "There was black smoke everywhere, explosions going off. It was horrific, both as a story and actually to do." Percy Sugden was one of the first on the scene, giving veteran actor Bill Waddington his most uncomfortable moment in his ten years on *Coronation Street*: "I had to rush down the street. It was hard running down the cobbles in my slippers; it was like running on hot coals. At the same time, I had to appear to be in a panic and it was a very hard move."

As Coronation Street filled with residents, inside the Rovers itself landlady Bet Lynch was woken by the commotion and, finding the bedroom full of smoke, tried to escape, crawling along the landing to the stairs. This sequence

DIRECTOR GARETH MORGAN WAS ADAMANT THAT REAL FIREMEN RATHER THAN ACTORS SHOULD PLAY THE FIRE-FIGHTERS. BILL WADDINGTON POSES WITH THE CREW.

was the most dangerous in the whole episode and Gareth Morgan is full of praise for actress Julie Goodyear, who insisted on going through with the scene when Bet finds her escape route cut off by flames, despite the risks: "The intensity of it really really worried me and I knew that she was frightened too, but she was adamant that she should do it. And it made the scene so much better, because she is such a well-known figure to the public that we couldn't really disguise somebody else."

The scene had to be recorded twice: the

MICHAEL LE VELL IS DIRECTED BY GARETH MORGAN AS HE PREPARES TO SMASH THE BEDROOM WINDOW.

Every precaution had been taken to ensure Bet's nightgown was flame-proof but the flames were stronger than anticipated. Julie Goodyear takes up the story: "Gareth was working so intently on getting the shot he wanted that he didn't notice the nightdress catch fire. I can assure you that the scream at the top of the staircase was authentic. As I finished, John Newman rushed in, picked me up and shouted 'Cut!'"

first time Gareth stopped the recording halfway through because the fire, completely out of control, was actually burning up the whole staircase before Julie reached it. The staircase had to be rebuilt and the sequence was recorded a week later; this time everyone knew the danger was real. Gareth sat in the control box, watching all the camera shots and directing the cameramen over headphones. Julie trusted him completely but was grateful to have the fire brigade and medical crew watching from behind the camera. The pyrotechnic experts ignited the fire and everyone waited as the sequence was carefully recorded.

At the back of Julie's mind was the memory of the flaming staircase: "It was real fear the second time; I'd seen what that fire could do. The fire brigade gave me oxygen every four minutes because the smoke was real."

The floor manager – the director's eyes and mouth on the studio floor – was John Newman. A burly Londoner, known for his strength, he kept a careful eye on Julie the whole time.

For the next scene, Bet Lynch had to crawl back into the bedroom and collapse on the floor. At this stage Julie called upon an incident from her past to make the scene more authentic: "When Laurence Olivier was working at Granada a while back he and I became friends. He was a good teacher and he taught me how to vomit. I had hoped that one day it would come in useful and I realised that someone in that situation would be sick, either from fear or from the fumes. I knew this was the time for it to be used."

Outside in Coronation Street, Kevin Webster climbed the ladder and prepared to smash his way into Bet's bedroom. He disappeared through the window just as the front windows of the pub were to blow out into the street, where the residents were standing. Gareth Morgan knew that this very tricky scene could only be done once: "There's always a worry about splintering glass and you can't do something like that with sugar glass because the heat would just melt the material before it actually blows out."

The cast members on the cobbles were told by Gareth what would happen; the pyrotechnic experts would explode the glass and at Gareth's command they would have to run as fast as possible away from the pub. At that point, any thought of the shoot being exciting was replaced by fear. For a scene involving such danger stand-ins would usually be used but these actors were so well known that there was no way the viewers would be fooled by someone dressed as Ken, Emily or Ivy.

Anne Kirkbride still recalls the countdown to the explosion with fear in her voice: "I was shaking all over and Bill Roache had to hold onto me to stop me running before the cue."

At Gareth's cue the glass blew, smoke billowed out and, screaming *en masse*, the cast fled over the cobbles and threw themselves onto the pavement. The shot was a success and remains one of the finest in the history of *Coronation Street*.

The next scene involved Kevin attempting to drag Bet to safety while the fire brigade started their rescue. The firemen were real and not actors. Michael Le Vell found this sequence the most exciting: "There was smoke everywhere and you couldn't see a thing. At one point I had to pick Bet off the floor and I couldn't see my hand in front of my face, let alone someone who was 15 feet away. I had to have every trust and confidence in the crew who were around us."

As Bet and Kevin were rescued by the fire brigade, the interior of the Rovers was dowsed down by the firemen. Part of *Coronation Street*'s history was dead – the Select and Snug would never be seen again – but the episode became a classic. The viewing figures of 21 million topped the ratings and the fire episode was repeated after the news that evening – a distinction never before bestowed on a drama programme.

Recently Gareth Morgan presented the cast with a memento of the fire – a decorative bottle which had been kept behind the old Rovers' bar since the first episode. It was the only prop to escape the fire at The Rovers Return.

THE PINEAPPLE PUB WAS LEFT COMPLETELY GUTTED BY THE PYROTECHNIC EXPERTS' SPECIALLY STAGED INFERNO.

LOCAL
PUBS & LANDLADIES

of this Parish

"You know them old paintings, where there's angels come out of the sky like and all rays of light and cupids wi' trumpets? It's a bit like that when Nellie Harvey walks in."

BET LYNCH

DURING their respective reigns, both Rovers' Queens, Annie Walker and Bet Gilroy, have had to suffer the unwelcome, but socially necessary, acquaintances in the business. Annie's tiger in a Persian-lamb coat was Nellie Harvey, who aspired to greater things and always commiserated with "Dear Anne" for having to rough it in a working-class pub. Bet, on the other hand, has had to enter Stella Rigby's lion den, or rather her self-contained villa in Tenerife, complete with own pool and maid service.

Along with Stella and Nellie, a few other licensees and barmaids have left their mark on the Street. Occasionally, the cameras have wandered away from the cobbles of Coronation Street to other hostelries in Weatherfield.

At the turn of the century, when the area was built, the brewery owned hundreds of small ale houses. Nearly every street had one on the corner, some had two. Names like "The Tripe Dressers Arms" and "The Davey Lamp" have become part of Weatherfield folklore. Some of these pubs still exist, many have been renovated, but sadly most have been demol-

ished. The brewery is building new pubs, many of them with themes – such as the threatened Yankees – but many of the customers fight against change. Brewery boss Sarah Ridley once told Annie Walker that the brewery had always produced beer for the working classes and their pubs must be for working-class men. Like Annie, Nellie Harvey and Stella Rigby would have cringed to hear their pubs referred to as "ale houses".

NELLIE HARVEY

As licensee of The Laughing Donkey, in Ondurman Street, Nellie Harvey felt a cut above her fellow licensed victuallers; The Donkey, as she liked to refer to the pub, overlooked the park and had its own beer garden. She was befriended by Annie Walker in 1965 when Annie sought backing in her attempt to be crowned chair of the Licensed Victuallers Association, Ladies Section. In those days, Nellie was a shining light in the organisation and willingly became Annie's patron. Her willingness had little to do with her confidence in

NELLIE
AND ANNIE'S FRIENDSHIP WAS A FRAGILE
TRUCE AT THE BEST OF TIMES.

Annie's abilities - she was attracted to Jack Walker and became his dancing partner at many brewery functions.

After Jack's death in 1970, Nellie became a more frequent visitor to The Rovers Return, where she and Annie tried to outdo each other, verbally and with possessions. When asked about her friendship with Mrs Harvey by Betty Turpin, Annie gave this insight into their relationship: "We never really have been . . . friends, as such, Nellie and I. Business associates, yes. And rivals. Oh, yes. Many's the time we've locked horns at the Lady Victuallers but that's always been monotonous really – I usually win."

Annie eventually gained the ultimate social edge on Nellie when she was made Mayoress of Weatherfield. Nellie was so envious she had to buy herself a new coat. She did all but beg an invite to the Mayoral ceremony but Annie refused to invite her, excusing herself by saying that all the invitations had been arranged weeks beforehand. Wanting to hit back and knock Annie off her social pedestal, Nellie made reference to the goings on at the Ogden's house, No.13: "I see they're fumigating down the road, dear. Such a novelty, there's not many places you see it done now." Without drawing breath Annie bounced back and, as always, had the last word: "Well, dear, as they say, there are none so pure as the purified."

The animosity between Annie and Nellie reached a peak in January 1974 when Nellie's downtrodden husband Arthur left her, stating that he intended to live with the only woman he had ever loved – the divine Annie. Annie was horrified when drunken Arthur arrived on her doorstep at midnight. Out of courtesy she took him in and let him sleep in the spare room in a pair of Billy's pyjamas. In the morning Arthur apologised and admitted he had drunk too much. His plans to return home were blighted when Nellie walked in and found them talking. Eyeing the pyjamas suspiciously, she told Annie she was welcome to him and would be hearing from her solicitor.

Annie, now Mayoress, was horrified at the thought of being involved in a divorce case and could not believe how she'd landed in such a position: "It's too ridiculous for words. A woman in my position. Of my reputation. Being accused of something so sordid."

She told Nellie not to blow things out of proportion but Nellie had a one-track mind: "How can I forgive you? Luring away my husband. Letting him cavort about your private quarters in pyjamas. If he's not been lured, I'm a Dutchman. Arthur's never cavorted in his life. And certainly never in pyjamas."

To Annie's horror, Nellie's mask of friendship dropped completely as she told her exactly what she'd always thought about her: "You're no friend of mine. You're just a condescending bitch. You stand there smiling and simpering and coming the great I-am as usual. While all you really are is Lady Muck!"

Although Arthur returned to Nellie, pleasing her by saying he didn't know what he'd ever seen in Annie, the bitter-sweet relationship between Nellie and Annie was never the same again. Annie sought out new friends within the LVA, landladies who shared her contempt for Madame Harvey.

ANNIE AND NELLIE ATTEMPTED TO OUTSHINE EACH OTHER WHEN THEY ENTERTAINED VISITING LV ETHNE WILLOUGHBY. NELLIE WAS PUT OUT WHEN ETHNE INVITED ANNIE TO VISIT HER CLASSY COUNTRY PUB.

A NEW ERA

When Bet Lynch inherited the throne vacated by Annie she did not have to wait long before the LVA came a-calling. This generation of landladies differed from Annie and Nellie in a number of ways – many held licences in their own names and took advantage of any opportunity to chat up the customers.

Bet found herself lured into a pretend friendship with domineering and scheming landlady Stella Rigby. They are still friends – in fact it is quite real now but over the years the relationship has suffered many knocks.

STELLA RIGBY

Like Nellie Harvey, Stella delights in taking any opportunity to remind Bet that she runs little more than a glorified ale house: "No detri-

STELLA RIGBY WAS READY TO BELIEVE ANYTHING OF BET – EVEN THAT SHE HAD SLEPT WITH HER HUSBAND.

ment to you Bet, because after all you can make a silk purse out of a sow's ear, but in a little back-street pub like this you don't get the cross-section, do you? I mean, take The White Swan. We get them from all walks of life. Architects. Businessmen. Chartered accountants..."

Stella's "little haunt", The White Swan, is situated on Clarence Street, one of the main busy commercial roads running through Weatherfield. She and her husband Paul run it together, although it's her name over the door: "Paul knows he'd be at the bus stop with his case packed if he tried taking liberties."

As soon as she first met Bet, Stella knew she was someone she needed to win over. She recognised her strength of character and saw in her a fighter who had risen through the ranks against the odds. Stella admired her for that but, of course, would never tell her so. Bet, meanwhile, took great care to keep her wits about her, recognising Stella and her cronies as powerful friends to have. She also knew they would make dangerous enemies: "It's like going for a paddle in a shark-infested pond."

Alec Gilroy knew Stella of old when he married Bet; he had worked for the brewery arranging pub entertainment for years. Like Bet, he had reservations about Stella's intentions whenever she came calling. Bet upset Alec by arranging a holiday with Stella when Alec had refused to take her on a honeymoon, claiming lack of funds. Alec was outraged at the thought of Bet and Stella swanning around North Africa: "That Stella Rigby, in Morocco . . . I tell you, she'll have blokes in nightshirts round her like flies round a jam pot. And they'll not go hungry, neither. She might not be a fully paid-up member of the nymphomaniac club, but she definitely helps them out when they're short-handed."

Whilst holidaying in Morocco, Bet and Stella struck up a genuine friendship. Away from the back-biting LVA crowd their professional admiration of each other blossomed into a friendship based on the knowledge that they were two of a kind. They were to spend many holidays together.

If Stella was a nymphomaniac, then her husband Paul was a lecherous, unfaithful womaniser. Stella was well aware of his reputation and began to be concerned when news reached her that Paul had been spending time at the Rovers. At that time Alec was away on business in the Middle East and Bet had become bored. Paul had escorted her to a few LV functions but Bet had managed to keep his wandering hands at bay. Stella decided to give Bet warning that she was aware of the situation and did not want it turning into something more sordid: "Paul is so transparent. He comes in with the milk stinking of drink and cheap scent. Honestly

Bet – these bits he gets with! I don't know where he digs them up, but from the smell of them they've passed their sell-by date on Woolworth's counter. He's got a horrible taste in women. Tarty, flashy and cheap. Still, why should I care? So long as he doesn't catch anything."

Confident that she had warned Bet off, Stella left her to her own devices with Paul. A few weeks later she was stunned to hear from Alec that he'd found Paul and Bet canoodling upon his return. Alec refused to believe that Bet had not been unfaithful and started divorce proceedings. Stella told him the idea was ridiculous but Alec knew Paul of old: "I've seen him in situations where you wouldn't have thought he was anybody's husband. Why can't he have been fratting with my wife? Have you got one of these little radio transmitters strapped to him? So you can follow his every move. Like they do with polar bears."

When Alec tried to call her bluff and told Stella that his staff could tell her about Paul and Bet's affair, Stella hardened. She had believed that Bet was too good a friend to sleep with her husband, but Alec had sowed sufficient doubt into her active mind for her to launch an attack on Bet: "I know I'm no angel. I don't know anybody who is. Not among our crowd. But there are rules. And one of 'em is keep your sticky hands off somebody else's husband. Even one like Paul. Don't forget Bet, I've seen you operate. Scores of times; all eyelashes and chest!" Finishing their friendship, Stella stormed out of the Rovers.

When Alec and Bet were reconciled, Alec admitted to Stella that he had been wrong and that Paul's friendship with Bet had been completely harmless. Stella was relieved but has never really trusted Bet since. She was secretly pleased to hear that Alec had left Bet, as she knew Bet had been taken down a peg – from landlady to manageress of the Rovers.

However, a common enemy has risen up in the trade – the dreaded Richard Willmore, area manager of all the local pubs. Stella feels more secure than Bet as she holds the licence of The White Swan, but she shared Bet's outrage when Liz McDonald was given the brewery's showpiece pub, The Queens. Liz, as well as being Bet's barmaid, had trained under Stella. Both Stella and Bet now realise they will be better off joining forces as the old crowd are being replaced by younger pub managers.

OTHER DRINKING ESTABLISHMENTS

When not drinking in The Rovers Return, the Street regulars have patronised two other local establishments. One, The Flying Horse, was built even before the Rovers; the other, The Graffiti, was opened in 1983. Both are run by the brewery and both have caused problems for the residents of Coronation Street.

THE FLYING HORSE

Situated on the corner of Jubilee Terrace and Clarence Street, The Flying Horse is a small ale house which was completely refurbished in 1984, including a mirrored bar. The pub was built in 1850 when the brewery, then Newton, Ridley &

Oakes, was just starting to open public houses. It was originally named The Flying Dutchman after the racehorse that won the 1849 Derby. The brewery renamed it The Flying Horse in 1905 for patriotic reasons.

Until the building of The Graffiti, The Flying Horse was the closest pub to the Rovers and many of the hard drinkers, like Stan Ogden, split opening hours between the two pubs. The regulars of both pubs clashed in "friendly" contests, such as tug-of-war, mixed football and pub olympics. The Rovers won most of the contests, although they lost a couple. In 1980, Fred Gee organised a barber-shop quartet against a foursome set up by Tony Hayes, landlord of The Flying Horse. The Rovers' team were soundly beaten as they were all singing off key. A couple of years before that Fred also lost another challenge, in a pram race to raise funds for the local hospital. It became serious business when the brewery promised a barrel of

LEN FAIRCLOUGH MADE A FOOL OF HIMSELF AS HE SWOONED OVER FLYING HORSE BARMAID ANITA REYNOLDS.

beer to the winning team. Fred was pushed in his pram by Gail Potter whilst Mavis Riley nearly strained herself pushing heavyweight Eddie Yeats. Suzie Birchall and Steve Fisher passed the finishing line first but were disqualified by steward Ena Sharples as Suzie had helped Steve drink the required pint at one of the pubs. A couple from The Flying Horse, Ted and Freda Loftus, were declared the winners and their pub won the barrel.

In 1978, Fred courted Flying Horse barmaid Alma Walsh. He wanted a pub of his own but the brewery were only taking on married landlords at the time. He had proposed marriage to

BET, HILDA AND VERA WAGED BATTLE AGAINST THE FLYING HORSE IN THE PUB OLYMPICS. HILDA WON WHEN VERA WAS DISQUALIFIED FOR CHEATING.

Betty Turpin and Bet Lynch but both turned him down. After running out of barmaids at the Rovers, lazy Fred started drinking at the nearest pub and decided Alma was a likely candidate. He did propose but Alma turned him down, explaining she'd had enough of the licensed trade and would not consider running a pub.

Fred was not the only Rovers regular to be attracted to the barmaids at The Flying Horse. In 1970, Len Fairclough neglected the Rovers in favour of champion darts player Anita Reynolds, who served at the Horse. He became serious about Anita despite the obvious age difference. She was a girl who was only interested in marriage and when he proposed she eagerly accepted. Unfortunately, he changed his mind the next day when he realised that they belonged to different genera-

SCHOOLGIRL JENNY BRADLEY AUDITIONS FOR ALEC, SINGING "WHAT I DID FOR LOVE" IN THE GRAFFITI BAR.

tions: her father had been at school with Stan Ogden! Telling Anita he had no serious intention of settling down, Len broke off the engagement.

Len's business partner Ray Langton was also attracted to The Flying Horse, in 1972 when Sandra Duffy served behind the bar. In order to impress Sandra, Ray entertained her in a luxury apartment he was refurbishing whilst the owner was abroad. Sandra fell for Ray, believing him to be wealthy, and felt used and humiliated when she discovered the truth. In revenge, she borrowed the keys from Ray and gave them to Franny Slater, a local villain who burgled the flat, stealing £5,000 in cash. Both Franny and Sandra fled the country, leaving Ray to face a police investigation.

The Flying Horse is now run by Marge Butler, a dark-haired floozy with a reputation of throwing parties after hours. In 1989, she employed Bet as barmaid when she had left Alec. Marge delighted in getting one up on Bet by sacking her on her second day, telling her she was a lousy barmaid. It was the realisation of the humiliation that Marge had caused Bet to suffer which moved Alec to be reconciled with his wife.

THE GRAFFITI

In 1983, business partners Mike Baldwin and Alec Yardley bought the disused Victorian warehouse on Rosamund Street and transformed it into a night-club, The Graffiti Club. It took Coronation Street by storm, with cars parking at all hours, noise and litter. No one was sad when the disco closed in 1984. The following year, Alec Gilroy, theatrical agent for the brewery, took over the members-only bar. For months he struggled to keep the till in profit, but then fate cast a kind blow to Alec. In June 1986 the Rovers was gutted by fire and the regulars looked for another watering hole. The Flying Horse was being refurbished so they moved, *en masse*, to Alec's grotty bar. Gloria Todd took a job behind the bar and Alec promised Jack Duckworth he'd employ him if he brought 40 new members into the bar. As well as serving ale at the Graffiti, Alec also held auditions at the pub and ran his agency from it.

When the Rovers reopened, Alec watched bitterly as his new customers left in droves. He tried to scupper Bet's new crew by poaching her barmaid Alison Dougherty, but his plan backfired when she ran off with the takings. Later on in the year, Alec gave up the bar to concentrate on his agency and the brewery closed it. The Graffiti still stands empty.

TIME GENTLEMEN PLEASE!

How the Rovers has altered

"When I'm gone they'll probably take the Rovers' facade brick by brick to a museum"

ANNIE WALKER

THE ROVERS RETURN INN has faced many changes over the years, the most important ones being the people who have lived and worked in the building. However, there have also been changes in the layout of the bar and living quarters and in the atmosphere of the pub.

Originally, the pub was sectioned off into three separate bars, although the only entrance into the pub was through the Public Bar. The smallest room, the Snug, was where unaccompanied women traditionally drank. Up to the First World War, this was the only room the women were allowed to be served in. Even in 1960, a sign in the Snug warned the ladies that they would be thrown out of the pub if they lingered at the bar. Pensioners like Ena, Minnie and Martha drank in the Snug because the drinks were a half-penny cheaper there than in the Public.

The other bar in the Rovers was the Select. This

THE NEW ROVERS' BAR HAS REMAINED UNCHANGED SINCE 1986. THE PHOTOGRAPHS ON THE WALL SHOW SCENES OF OLD WEATHERFIELD.

THE ROVERS' SNUG WAS HOME TO ENA SHARPLES AND
HER CRONIES, MINNIE CALDWELL AND MARTHA
LONGHURST. THEY SPENT THEIR EVENINGS THERE AS IT
WAS CHEAPER THAN HEATING THREE HOUSES.

room was reached via a small corridor along the
side of the Snug. It doubled as the Street's
function room - complete with stage area - and
a room where patrons could drink in private
away from the crowds, paying a penny more for
their drinks and waitress service. Hardly anyone used the facility.

At Christmas the Select would be thrown
open to everyone for shows and sing-songs.
Memorable moments include Minnie Caldwell
reciting "The Owl And The Pussy Cat" at a
party in 1969 (she could not remember more
than the first verse) and Rita Littlewood's
impersonation of Marlene Dietrich in a 1972
show. Rita, a professional singer, also appeared
a year later in a show put on by the local ladies
as a forfeit for losing a bowls' match. The only
problem was that the ladies had to present the
cabaret in drag. There were boos and hisses
when Rita walked on stage in a glittering dress
and blonde wig but the men roared with laughter when she announced, in a husky voice, that
she was Danny LaRue. The last show to be put
on in the Select was the 1984 talent show, in
which Percy Sugden presented his terrible
farm-yard impressions and Alf Roberts told
awful jokes.

The Public was the largest of the three bars,

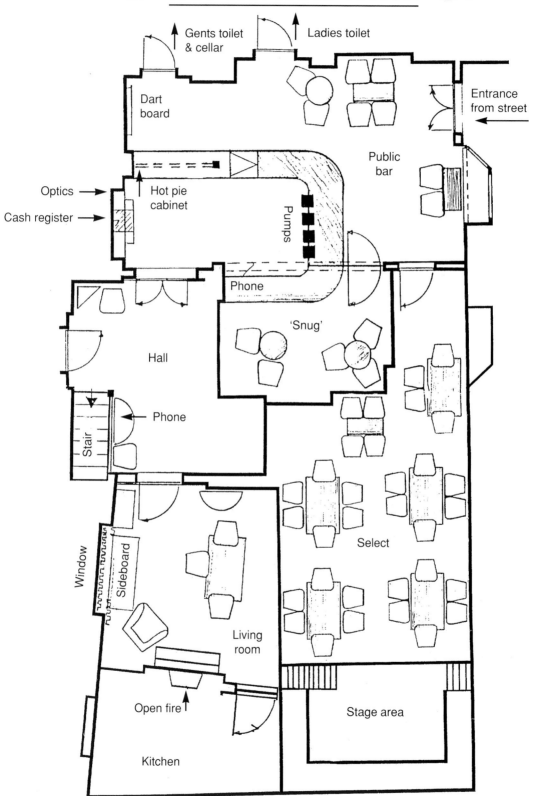

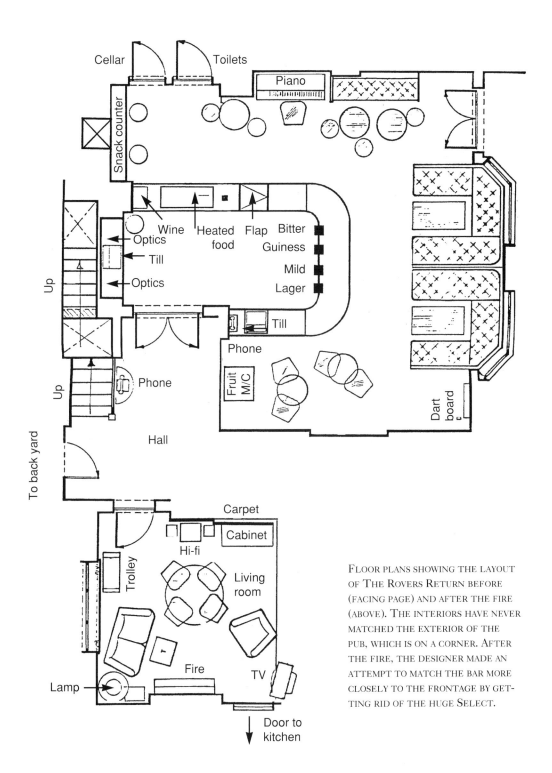

Cellar

Toilets

Piano

Snack counter

Up

Wine

Optics

Till

Optics

Heated food

Flap

Bitter

Guiness

Mild

Lager

Till

Phone

Up

Phone

Fruit M/C

Hall

Dart board

To back yard

Carpet

Cabinet

Hi-fi

Trolley

Living room

Fire

TV

Lamp

Door to kitchen

FLOOR PLANS SHOWING THE LAYOUT OF THE ROVERS RETURN BEFORE (FACING PAGE) AND AFTER THE FIRE (ABOVE). THE INTERIORS HAVE NEVER MATCHED THE EXTERIOR OF THE PUB, WHICH IS ON A CORNER. AFTER THE FIRE, THE DESIGNER MADE AN ATTEMPT TO MATCH THE BAR MORE CLOSELY TO THE FRONTAGE BY GETTING RID OF THE HUGE SELECT.

furnished with cast-iron tables and wooden chairs, although most of the regulars preferred to stand at the bar, chatting to the staff. Two doors led off from the Public, one to the gents and the cellar, the other to the ladies' lavatory. There was also a trap-door to the cellar behind the bar, but this was rarely used.

Space behind the Rovers' bar was at a pre-mium until 1964 when a wooden cupboard, used for storing glasses, was removed from the middle of the floor. The cupboard had always been in the way and the barmaids were forever complaining that the splintered wood kept lad-dering their stockings, as they tried to squeeze round it.

In 1961, Annie Walker made reference to

the fact that the pub needed complete renovation and drew up plans for alterations, which included knocking the three bars into one. She faced huge opposition from her husband and customers, who liked the pub the way it was, and the idea was dropped. The pub had always been a working-man's local and the traditional sawdust had only been removed from the floor as late at 1957, along with the spittoons that had stood along the bar since 1902.

The three-bar system remained in operation until that fateful night in June 1986 when the Rovers was gutted by fire. The pub was then completely refurbished by the brewery and the three bars were knocked into one large one. The other big change in the layout was in the hall of the private quarters. The fire had caused so much damage to the staircase that a new one was built going in the opposite direction.

In 1992, the Rovers' kitchen was condemned by the Health Inspector and was completely modernised to meet the requirements of new legislation. This has also allowed a larger selection of bar meals to be served.

Another change took place in May 1993 when bar pumps were installed behind the bar. The last bar pumps to be seen in the Rovers were taken out in 1968, but now real ale has returned to the pub, to comply with the new licensing laws which require pubs to offer a larger range of beers to their customers.

One thing has remained constant at the Rovers: customers are always guaranteed a friendly welcome, a shoulder to cry on and scintillating conversation from the likes of barmaid Raquel Wolstenhulme - "I were always led to believe I were equally good at most things. I were told that when I were at school. They said - 'Raquel - you have no particular talents.' I can turn my hand to owt, me."

LEFT: THE CAMERA MOVES INTO THE OLD PUBLIC BAR AS PAT PHOENIX STRIKES A TYPICAL ELSIE TANNER POSE.

RIGHT: ANNIE HAD ALWAYS WANTED TO KNOCK THE THREE BARS INTO ONE, BUT THIS WASN'T DONE UNTIL AFTER HER RETIREMENT.

WHAT'S YOUR TIPPLE?

"Three milk stouts and make sure there's no lipstick on the glasses"

ENA SHARPLES

"I'm afraid we don't serve 'the usual' in here; we've got bitter, lager, mild and a whole range of spirits."

JACK DUCKWORTH

*T*HE DRINKS SELECTION at The Rovers Return has grown dramatically over the past 32 years. In 1960 the Walkers offered the brewery's mild and bitter on tap but all other drinks were bottled. Men drank pints, the women were offered gin or vodka and the pensioners bought the cheaper bottled stout. There was one optic, dispensing brandy. All other spirits were kept in bottles around the till at the back of the bar. Annie Walker kept miniature liqueur bottles on the top shelf. On Christmas Day 1961, Annie berated Jack for opening a miniature of cherry brandy: "You know I like to keep my miniatures for display purposes only." Other bottled drinks, such as lager, shandy and cider, were kept on shelves under the bar, along with minerals, fruit juices and lemonade.

Nowadays, the Rovers boasts a bar overflowing with variety. Draft bitter, mild and lager from the brewery are available, as well as other guest beers. Optics holding bottles of all kinds of spirits hang on the wall behind the till and the shelves are crammed with bottles of liqueurs, spirits and minerals. As well as hot and cold meals, fresh coffee is available throughout the day and Bet has a book behind the bar telling her how to make exotic cocktails. A major change is that customers can no longer buy cigarettes in the pub.

The Rovers has always stocked a good supply of sherry. As well as being Annie Walker's favourite drink, she liked to pass it round at times of celebration. However, it is only in the last fifteen years that wine has been on offer. When Annie fought Renee Bradshaw's application for an off-licence, she blamed her defeat solely on Bet. When questioned about wine sales, Bet told the court that they kept bottles of wine up to a pound but if something more exotic was

LEFT: EVERY EVENING, ANNIE AND JACK WOULD SET THE MILK STOUTS OUT ON THE SNUG COUNTER IN READINESS FOR THE EVER-PREDICTABLE ENA, MINNIE AND MARTHA.

NEWTON & RIDLEY'S TWO MOST POPULAR BOTTLED DRINKS – LAGER AND PALE ALE – FAVOURED BY HILDA OGDEN.

wanted she would send out to an off-licence! Annie was not amused, but the court was.

Drinking habits have changed in the Rovers, just as the clientele has changed. Heavy drinkers, such as Len Fairclough, Ray Langton and Stan Ogden, have made way for the more health-conscious regulars. Taxi-driver Don Brennan refuses to drink anything stronger than fruit juice when he's working but Angie Freeman would have caused a stir in the 1960s Rovers with her favourite drink of draught bitter.

Some of the old regulars

ABOVE: IN THE EARLY 1960S THE CUSTOMERS WERE HEAVY DRINKERS. ALBERT TATLOCK, LEN FAIRCLOUGH AND FRANK BARLOW WOULD NEVER HAVE TOUCHED LAGER OR ORANGE JUICE, AS THEIR 1990S COUNTERPARTS DO.

AT PARTIES IN THE ROVERS, THE STAFF BREAK FREE AND DRINK WHATEVER IS TO HAND.

were strongly identified with what they used to drink. The three old ladies in the Snug – Ena, Minnie and Martha – drank milk stout; Albert Tatlock was partial to a rum (but only when someone else was paying); Annie Walker kept her own decanter full of medium sherry; and Hilda Ogden enjoyed a small British port and lemon (or as Alec Gilroy referred to it – "a Grimsby"). Elsie Tanner drank nothing but gin and tonic. When, in 1979, Ivy Tilsley ordered an "Elsie Tanner" Bet knew exactly what to serve her.

But what of today's regulars? The following list shows their favourite tipples:

Landlady Bet Gilroy enjoys a gin a tonic.

Raquel Wolstenhulme	*Pineapple juice or shandy*
Betty Turpin	*Medium Sherry*
Deirdre Barlow	*Lager*
Emily Bishop	*Medium Sherry*
Percy Sugden	*Half of mild*
Ivy Brennan	*Lager or gin and tonic*
Don Brennan	*Bitter or orange juice*
Curly Watts	*Bitter*
Jack Duckworth	*Bitter*
Vera Duckworth	*Lager, shandy or gin*
Jim McDonald	*'Pint of wallop'*
Liz McDonald	*Gin and tonic*
Steve McDonald	*Bitter*
Andy McDonald	*Bitter*
Kevin Webster	*Bitter*
Sally Webster	*Lager*
Ken Barlow	*Mild*
Reg Holdsworth	*Red wine or bitter*
Rita Sullivan	*Vodka and tonic*
Martin Platt	*Bitter*
Gail Platt	*Fruit juice or lager*
Des Barnes	*Bitter or red wine*
Derek Wilton	*Half of bitter*
Mavis Wilton	*Sweet sherry or fruit juice*
Denise Osbourne	*White wine and soda*
Mike Baldwin	*Scotch*
Alma Baldwin	*Gin and tonic*
Alf Roberts	*Bitter*
Audrey Roberts	*Gin and tonic*
Phyllis Pearce	*Pale ale*

THE REAL BARTENDER

Jim Coyle has been set dresser on *Coronation Street* for the last two and a half years. It is his job to maintain the Rovers set every week, keeping it clean and restocking the bar with both drink and food. While Raquel and Bet rush around behind the bar serving customers on screen, Jim ensures that all their props are ready for them and in exactly the right position. When the cameras stop, Jim moves in to restock the shelves, reheat the hotpot, polish the tables and test the beer – in fact he is Tina Fowler, Betty Turpin, Hilda Ogden and Jack Duckworth all rolled into one!

Jim is responsible for making sure the characters are served the correct drinks. However, he is quick to point out that nothing is what it seems on screen. Actors in a Rovers scene may have to replay the scene as many as ten times to ensure that what is seen on screen is perfect. If a character had to drink a pint of bitter each time the scene was shot, the actor would end up very drunk if the beer were real.

The only real drinks served behind the Rovers bar are minerals and fruit juices – everything else is false. The bitter is shandy and the lager is even more heavily diluted with lemonade. The spirits are concocted by Jim in his prop room – if a customer orders a dark drink, such as brandy or whisky what is actually served is a mixture of burnt sugar and water. The clear spirits – vodka and gin – are just plain water. There are occasional exceptions to the rule: if a character were to order a one-off drink which could not be faked, such as egg flip, then the real drink would be served.

Whenever Mike Baldwin orders a scotch in the pub he does not receive the usual burnt sugar as actor Johnny Briggs dislikes the taste, so he is served apple juice from a special optic instead.

THE STARS
BEHIND THE BAR

DORIS SPEED

*"I don't think Annie's a snob, but I don't think she can accept the fact
that she is working in a slum pub. She has aspirations for better things.
People like her are necessary, otherwise nothing would get done."*

DORIS appeared in the first episode of *Coronation Street* in December 1960. She made her last appearance as Annie in October 1983, in Episode 3351. During her 23 years in the series she appeared in a staggering 1746 episodes. She rates fifth highest in the league of episodes played, topped only by Ken Barlow, Emily Bishop, Len Fairclough and Bet Gilroy. Not bad for someone who thought she was signing up for a 16 episode series!

She was born into a showbusiness family –father was a singer, George Speed, her mother Ada was an actress. Doris toured with her parents from a very early age, travelling everywhere with them

DORIS SPEED AT HOME IN THE ROVERS (LEFT) AND LENDING A HAND DURING THE BULLDOZING OF THE OLD *CORONATION STREET* LOT IN 1982 (RIGHT).

in a Moses basket. She made her first appearance on stage aged three – as a flaxen-haired child singing a song about a golliwog. Her first real part came when she was five, when she played the Infant Prince of Rome in a Victorian melodrama called *The Royal Divorce*.

As she travelled with her parents, she never went to school regularly. Each Monday morning her mother would take her to the local town hall to get her a place at a nearby school, and every weekend the troupe – along with Doris – moved on to the next town and school. At 14, Doris started typing and shorthand to help pay the rent, but, encouraged by her parents, she joined a repertory company in the north and progressed to BBC radio. Her voice was featured in many

radio programmes – stories, features, plays and children's programmes.

From radio Doris drifted into television, working as a stooge for comedians. In 1960, she was working in a play in Bristol when she was asked to attend an audition in Manchester for a new serial. She refused, saying it was impossible. The casting department at Granada persisted and eventually – in a foul temper – Doris auditioned for *Coronation Street*. She was the 58th potential Annie Walker seen and was given the part on the spot.

The success of *Coronation Street* did not change Doris. She bought a small semi-detached house in Manchester and saved her money rather than indulging in an extravagant lifestyle. Her mother lived with her until her death in the early 1970s at the age of 97.

Annie brought many accolades for Doris, including honorary membership of the Licensed Victuallers' Association, the 1979 Pye Television award for an outstanding contribution to television and, in 1977, an MBE.

Ill-health forced Doris to leave the series in 1983. Shortly afterwards her house was raided by thugs and all her possessions were either wrecked or stolen. The shock was too much for Doris, and she sold her beloved home and moved into a private nursing home in Bury. She still lives at the home and has recently made public appearances. In 1992, she publicised a *Coronation Street* book, *Weatherfield Life*, and later the same year appeared as a guest on *Classic Coronation Street*.

SINCE LEAVING *CORONATION STREET*, DORIS SPEED HAS RETURNED TO VISIT FRIENDS. IN 1988 SHE OPENED THE STREET TO THE PUBLIC ON THE FIRST OF GRANADA'S TOURS.

ARTHUR LESLIE

"Fans always seem surprised to find the characters of Jack Walker and my own are almost identical. The reason is that, unlike most of the cast, I'm not assuming the character, but playing myself."

ARTHUR LESLIE was the first of the *Coronation Street* family to die. His death, on 30 June 1970, shattered not only his friends at Granada but also the millions of fans who had watched his portrayal of Jack Walker since Episode 2. His funeral, at Lytham Crematorium, was attended by the cast and two thousand fans, many weeping openly for a man they had grown to love.

As gentlemanly, friendly Jack Walker,

Arthur Leslie was hugely popular with the audience. His long-suffering relationship with Annie won him the admiration of men and women alike. His portrayal of mine host was so lifelike that when the programme first started many viewers believed he was actually a publican. In fact, Arthur Leslie had never served behind a real-life bar.

He was born in Newark, where his parents were playing at the local theatre. Born Arthur Broughton (his son Anthony Broughton recently played the part of shopkeeper Les Curry in *Coronation Street*), Arthur started his own theatrical career in 1916, in rep at the Queen's Theatre in Farnworth. He married

FOR TEN YEARS, ARTHUR LESLIE TRAVELLED TO AND FROM THE GRANADA STUDIOS ON THE TRAIN, SURPRISING THE FANS WHO SPOTTED HIM *EN ROUTE*.

AFTER A HARD DAY WORKING IN FRONT OF THE CAMERA, ARTHUR LESLIE USED TO UNWIND BEHIND THE CAMERA.

placid type of man who is prepared to put up with almost any amount of nagging from his wife, Annie, before finally he is forced to put his foot down."

In his spare time Arthur Leslie turned his hand to movie-making. In the 1950s he ran his own repertory company in Leigh, at the Theatre Royal, for 97 weeks. Before appearing in *Coronation Street*, he played a number of small roles on television and was actually planning to retire when he auditioned for the part of Jack. Fortunately for the series and his fans, he continued working for a further ten years.

actress Betty Morton Powell after they met while acting together in a play in Rotherham. Arthur Leslie once commented about his happy marriage: "My real wife has all the good characteristics to be seen in Annie without any of those bad ones like snobbishness."

The believability of Jack Walker came from Arthur's complete understanding of his on-screen character: "Jack is the genial,

ANTHONY BROUGHTON TOASTS HIS FATHER ARTHUR LESLIE DURING HIS SHORT TIME ON *CORONATION STREET*, IN MAY 1993, WHEN HE PLAYED GROCER LES CURRY.

KENNETH FARRINGTON

"I realised very early on that I would get bored if I stayed in the series for too long. I gain by leaving – I can do other roles, and they gain because I come back fresh to the part."

EVERY *CORONATION STREET* actor brings something of themselves to the characters they play. For example, Elsie Tanner's wayward son Dennis was created as a petty thief and shady character; however, Philip Lowrie, the actor who played him, brought considerable charm to the character and excuses were made for Dennis' criminal activities – everyone considered that he was easily led, rather than a nasty piece of work. However, the character of Dennis could have taken another route, one much closer to the original intentions, as Kenneth Farrington was very nearly cast in the role.

Both Kenneth and Philip were screen tested and Philip won the role – which ran for eight years. However, the producers were so taken by Kenneth's moody interpretation of Dennis that they created a role for him – that of publican's son, Billy Walker. Over the years – he first appeared in Episode 15 and last appeared nine years ago in Episode 2471 – Billy changed from ambitious teenager to blackmailing rogue.

Kenneth Farrington was born in London and joined *Coronation Street* after leaving RADA. Billy first appeared for only seven months; when he left, Kenneth spent the next three years in theatre. His love of the theatre extends beyond acting on stage: in the mid-1970s he directed plays in Manchester theatres, one of them featuring his screen fiancée, Deirdre Hunt, actress Anne Kirkbride.

Always a private person, Ken Farrington never enjoyed the fame that came with being part of *Coronation Street* and always found it hard working in Manchester while his family stayed in London. For 23 years Billy Walker

THE ROLE OF BILLY WALKER WAS CREATED ESPECIALLY FOR KEN FARRINGTON AFTER HE HAD IMPRESSED THE PRODUCERS.

was the rover who always returned. Sometimes he would not appear for years and then suddenly pop up, usually in financial trouble. His longest stretch in the series was from 1970 to 1974. Each time Billy left the show, it was in response to Ken's desire to return to the theatre. Although he had many friends in the programme, he became restless with the studio system and longed for a live audience.

As well as theatre, Ken has appeared in many television shows. He has recently been seen in episodes of *The Bill*, *Grange Hill* and *Trainer*.

ROY BARRACLOUGH

"I think Alec's a monster. I can't see any of myself in Alec at all, but he's fun to play. I like him better when he's hard, it's easier to play comedy, but I don't like opting for the easy way out."

WHEN ROY BARRACLOUGH bid farewell to the Street in 1992 he left a big gap at the Rovers. For six years he had regularly portrayed Alec Gilroy, five of those years as the husband of Bet Lynch. The Gilroys' love match was one of the *Coronation Street*'s major attractions – his penny-pinching ways, her determined extravagance and their superb one-liners.

Roy first appeared as Alec in 1972, for two episodes. He did a further two in 1975 as Rita Littlewood's theatrical agent. As well as playing Alec he also featured as four other minor parts in the programme.

Roy was born in Dodgson Road, Preston. He trained as a draughtsman at a technical college, and his first job was at a foundry. However, ever since he was a child Roy had been interested in show business. He made puppet theatres at home and joined a church drama group. Later he joined the Preston Drama Club and spent his spare time watching the local repertory company at the Hippodrome Theatre. In 1957 he landed his first professional role – as a pupil in *The Headmaster*. He was paid £2 for a week's work and was completely smitten. After gaining his Higher National Diploma he made the big

ALEC GILROY BECAME THE FIFTH LICENSEE OF THE ROVERS IN 1987. ROY BARRACLOUGH NEVER INTENDED TO STAY IN THE SERIES FOR LONG.

MANY SCENES IN THE ROVERS HAD TO BE RECORDED AGAIN AND AGAIN AS THE ACTORS FOUND IT HARD TO KEEP A STRAIGHT FACE AROUND COMIC ROY.

decision and dumped his job to become an entertainment manager at a holiday camp on the Isle of Wight.

Nita Valerie (she once screen-tested for the role of Ena Sharples) took Roy on at the repertory company she ran in Huddersfield. He became an assistant stage manager but, after

"THAT WOMAN FROM ROSAMUND STREET - THE ONE WITH THE VEINS AND NECK BRACE - SAID YOU MIGHT BE TAKING ON STAFF FOR THE HOLIDAYS": ADA SHUFFLEBOTTOM (ALIAS LES DAWSON) TACKLES ALEC GILROY.

two weeks, was promoted to character actor. Oldham Rep followed and he soon found himself acting in front of the television cameras, mainly for Yorkshire Television and Granada.

He made his first appearance in *Coronation Street* in 1965 as a tour guide, showing the residents around the Blue John mines. Shortly afterwards he joined the late Les Dawson and created the marvellous "Cissie and Ada" sketches. To celebrate *Coronation Street*'s 30th anniversary Les joined Roy in a sparkling spectacular to play homage to the Rovers.

Since leaving *Coronation Street*, Roy has appeared, non-stop, in the theatre. When he left, he moved straight into a new play *Feed* at Bolton's Octagon Theatre. The play was written Tom Elliott, a stalwart of *Coronation Street*'s writing team and a close friend of Roy's. He has also appeared in pantomime - as the dame – and has recently toured in *Sherlock Holmes: The Musical* – as Dr Watson.

JULIE GOODYEAR

*"Being in the Street has given me somewhere
to belong, as a person."*

CLAD IN A TIGHT BLACK DRESS with a plunging neckline, Julie Goodyear pulled her first pint as Bet Lynch. It was November 1970 and Julie had been in the long-running series for six months. It was her second stint in the series – Bet had first appeared in 1966 as a local factory-worker.

Julie was born in Heywood, Lancashire, where her parents ran The Bay Horse public house. On leaving school she had joined the typing pool at the local aircraft factory and married draughtsman Ray Sutcliffe. Julie was 17 at the time and deeply in love. She was devastated when Ray emigrated to Canada a year later, leaving her with a baby son Gary. Julie supported Gary by working in offices and selling appliances door-to-door. She managed to save money for a modelling course and her modelling eventually led to television work.

The part of Bet the machinist was her first acting role. Julie was thrilled to be in her favourite programme, as were her parents, Alice and William Goodyear: "My parents were very proud of me joining the *Street*, they watched every episode. It was a wonderful feeling, becoming a part of it all, but dreadful when the role came to a end."

She had appeared in six episodes but she knew she lacked the experience she needed to become a successful actress. Pat Phoenix

LEFT: WITH DIANA
DAVIES AND BETTY
DRIVER, JULIE SANG
IN A 1972 CHRISTMAS
SPECIAL. A GOOD
SINGER, JULIE HAD
TO SING OFF KEY ON
PURPOSE FOR THE
OCCASION.

RIGHT: *CORONATION
STREET* HAS ALWAYS
BEEN A SECOND
HOME FOR JULIE.

JULIE WITH HER BELOVED MOTHER ALICE GOODYEAR. ALICE ALWAYS TOOK GREAT PLEASURE IN HER DAUGHTER'S ACHIEVEMENTS.

advised Julie to train in repertory theatre and she joined Oldham Rep. More television work at Granada followed. She appeared in *Nearest and Dearest*, *The Dustbinmen* and Tony Warren's *The War of Darkie Pilbeam*.

Julie picks up her story: "I did an episode of *Family At War* for June Howson, who was due to take over as producer of *Coronation Street*, and she asked if I would be interested in becoming a regular member of the cast. I really didn't take the question seriously because it was my dream and sometimes when dreams come true you find it very hard to believe that it's happening. But true to her word, a contract came." It was May 1970 when Bet walked down the cobbled street again, and she has remained ever since.

In 1973 Julie married again. The groom was businessman Tony Rudman. Julie was escorted to the church in Bury by her son Gary, and soldiers from the King's Own Border Regiment formed a guard of honour with fixed bayonets. The cast of *Coronation Street* attended the wedding and outside the church thousands of fans blocked the road. What they didn't see were the events at the reception when Julie's new husband walked out of the room and never returned. Julie's second marriage had ended and was soon annulled.

Julie married a third time – to American airline executive Richard Skrob – but their work commitments meant that the couple were seldom together, as she was filming in England while he ran his business in California, and they divorced after a year. A few years later he died of leukaemia. Julie says she feels no animosity or bitterness towards any of her husbands.

In 1979, Julie was told she had cervical cancer. It had been detected during a routine smear test and Julie prayed that she had not left it too late to have the cancerous cells removed. Fortunately for Julie and her millions of fans, she hadn't. Fellow actor Peter Adamson (the *Street*'s Len Fairclough) sat by Julie's bedside in hospital as she recovered from her successful operation. Representing all Julie's friends in the cast, Peter whispered precious words of comfort and love. As soon as she was well enough Julie launched an appeal for funds for Manchester's Christie Hospital. In September 1983, the Julie Goodyear Laboratory was opened at the hospital, much to the actress' pride. She has never stopped campaigning and urging women to take regular smears. Tragically, Julie's mother died of cancer in 1987.

When Bet took over The Rovers Return in January 1985, many people commented that she was to be the new Annie Walker. Julie has always disputed this: "There could never be a replacement for Annie Walker. She was an original. My character is nothing like the character of Annie Walker. When an actress like Doris has done their job to such a high standard you can never step into their shoes, you can only stand next to them."

Julie is known amongst the *Coronation Street* crew for being a perfectionist, not only in her work, but in her environment. She looks upon her job of running the Rovers' bar as a huge responsibility: "It has to be sparkling, the glasses have to be clean, pumps have to work. The living-room set is also my responsibility. I don't allow people to sit about in it; it's a working set, and I don't want props moved. That can sometimes come across as me being a difficult person, but that's the only way I can do my job. Before I start recording I always check both those sets. Every week, to the finest detail."

Beverley Callard, the *Street*'s Liz McDonald, now a landlady in her own right, fondly remembers her first scenes in the Rovers. She was very daunted by the idea of working in the pub and is grateful for all the advice Julie Goodyear gave her: "Julie was absolutely fantastic when I first started in the Rovers. I can

remember her showing me around the set for the first time. She said 'you put your money here, take the money as you say your lines, write on your script "Mike Baldwin will have a large scotch and Alma drinks a G&T" and in the end you remember, as a barmaid would, what the regulars drink."

Big-hearted Julie has always sought out love – just as her screen character Bet has. She still lives in Heywood, and has never let stardom go to her head. She is now a doting grandmother: Gary has two children – Emily Alice and Elliott; Emily is named after Julie's deeply missed mother.

BOLD, BLONDE AND BRASSY - THE INIMITABLE BET LYNCH.

BETTY

Queen of the Hotpot

"There's an awful lot of Betty Turpin in me."

BETTY DRIVER

BETTY TURPIN is the Rovers' longest-serving barmaid. Since 1969 she has pulled pints with a cheerful smile, a merry quip and a heart-warming laugh. In her twenty-four years behind the bar she has appeared in 1668 episodes, with most of her scenes played in the Rovers. During that time she has served count-less pints and hotpots to a whole range of characters and actors. When the cameras stop rolling, jovial Betty Turpin is replaced by equally jovial Betty Driver.

To Betty Driver the role of Mrs Turpin came at a time when she had already had a successful career and had thought she had finished with showbusiness. From an early age, Betty earned her living by singing. At 14 she hit the newspaper headlines when she sang at London's Prince of Wales Theatre; it was her first appearance in the capital and she received a standing ovation. The same year she appeared in *Mr Tower of London*, making her the youngest leading lady in the country.

At 18 Betty joined Henry Hall's famous Dance Orchestra, touring with him all around the country for six years, during which time she made hundreds

ARTHUR LESLIE PROVIDED GREAT ENCOURAGEMENT AS HE SUPPORTED BETTY DURING HER FIRST SCENES IN THE ROVERS.

BETTY HAS FOND MEMORIES OF DORIS
SPEED'S WIT AND SENSE OF HUMOUR.

of television and radio appearances. She quickly became one of the most popular vocalists in the country, with hits including "Sailor with the Navy Blue Eyes". At one stage she had her own television show *A Date With Betty* and appeared in British films such as *Penny Paradise*, *Let's Be Famous*, and *Facing the Music*.

As well as pursuing her singing career, Betty branched out as a straight actress. She soon discovered she had a flair for comedy as well and a whole new world opened up. Betty was first considered for a role in *Coronation Street* in 1964 when she was auditioned for the part of Hilda Ogden. However, she had to pass up the part as she was contracted to a large soap powder company at the time, starring in a series of television commercials. Once the contract finished, she was snatched up by Granada Television to play opposite Arthur Lowe in *Pardon the Expression*, a spin-off from *Coronation Street*. Unfortunately Betty slipped in the studio while filming a complicated scene and injured her spine. At that time she thought it was to be the end of her acting career.

In 1967, Betty took over a public house with her sister Freda. It was there, two years later, that *Coronation Street* producer Harry Kershaw asked her to join the series as Betty, the new barmaid, a part he wanted to write for her. Hugely flattered, Betty agreed. However, it was a long while since she had acted and last-minute nerves threatened to ruin her chance of a new career: "I'd had a throat operation and hardly had any voice at all. I was so nervous coming into a show that was so well established. My first scenes were with dear Arthur Leslie, who played Jack Walker, and he said 'don't be nervous Betty.' But I said 'you're all speaking in quite good voices, I haven't got much of a voice.' He said 'Don't worry, I'll be there all the time.' He had his hand on my back every time I did a line, to give me confidence. He was wonderful and asked the boys on the boom to bring the boom up close every time I spoke, so it was never noticed. Arthur really got me through my first weeks and I worshipped him for that."

Sadly, Arthur Leslie died shortly afterwards. In the storylines, Annie took over the helm of the pub, with Betty taking more responsibility as her senior barmaid. Betty Driver's memories of Doris Speed are dominated by the fun, humorous side to her personality: "She was wonderful fun to act with but had one annoying habit. She used to clear all the props away after rehearsals. During a take you would go forward to the bar and you couldn't find any props! You'd have to stop and ask what had happened to them; Doris would have moved them all to one side, saying she didn't like clutter. She was lovely to work with."

Although she had run two pubs in real life,

Betty found the Rovers hard to adjust to: "The pubs that I had run had long bars and were rather spacious, but the Rovers was so tiny. I couldn't understand why the sets were so weeny; they looked so big when they were on the screen."

One similarity, however, between real pubs and the Rovers is the amount of work needed behind the bar. Scenes in the pub tend to be very long, full of characters and extras. Between saying their saying lines, these actors can drink and stand around together chatting and waiting for cues. The bar staff, on the other hand, have to rush about serving, pulling pints, opening bottles, feeding the till and serving food, as well as having to smile at customers, give the right change and remember lines!

The role of barmaid in *Coronation Street*'s Rovers Return must be one of the hardest jobs in television. Even scenes when the staff are standing chatting at the till can be strenuous, as Betty comments: "Today I've done a scene where I had to put money in the till, the float.

Money is so dirty to handle and we did it time and time again. You can see five pence pieces and ten pences floating before your eyes!"

Betty Driver has loved every moment of her time in the programme and has had the privilege of working with some truly wonderful actors. She does, however, have one regret: "Years ago I felt I would have liked to have run the Rovers but now it doesn't bother me. You bed down into a character. But originally I would have liked to have run the pub. Still, I really enjoy myself and love playing Betty, so it doesn't matter."

Betty's hotpot is nearly as famous as The Rovers Return. Betty first served it in 1973 when the pub was under the management of Glyn Thomas. He put food on the menu to encourage people to spend more money over the bar. Betty defied his command to make it salty (to make the customers more thirsty) and served a hotpot her mother used to make. Since then she has changed the recipe a few times but is now confident that she has perfected it. The regulars all agree with her and you are more than welcome to try the recipe for yourself.

BOTH BETTY DRIVER AND JULIE GOODYEAR ARE PROUD TO SAY THAT AFTER 23 YEARS OF WORKING TOGETHER THEY HAVE NEVER HAD A CROSS WORD.

BETTY'S HOTPOT

1 ½ LB (675 G) NECK OF LAMB, CUBED
1 ½ LB (675 G) POTATOES, PEELED AND THINLY SLICED
1 LARGE OR 2 MEDIUM ONIONS, ROUGHLY CHOPPED
¾ PINT (425 ML) LIGHT STOCK OR HOT WATER
1 TABLESPOON WORCESTERSHIRE SAUCE
1 BAYLEAF
1 TABLESPOON FLOUR
1 OZ (25G) DRIPPING AND 1OZ (25 G) BUTTER
OR 2 OZ (50 G) BUTTER
SALT AND PEPPER TO SEASON

Preheat the oven to 170°C/325°F/gas mark 5.

Melt the dripping or 1 oz (25 g) butter over a high heat in a heavy-bottomed frying pan until the fat smokes. Seal the meat and continue frying until nicely browned. Remove the pieces from the pan to a deep casserole or divide among four individual high-sided, ovenproof dishes.

Turn down the heat to medium. Fry the onions in the pan juices, adding a little more butter or dripping if necessary. When the onions are soft and starting to brown, sprinkle on the flour and stir in to soak up the fat and the juices. As the flour paste starts to colour, start adding stock or water a few tablespoons at a time, stirring vigorously to avoid lumps. Gradually add the rest of the liquid. Bring to a simmer, stirring constantly, add the Worcestershire sauce and season with salt and pepper to taste.

Pour the onions and liquid over the meat and mix well. Tuck in the bayleaf (tear into four pieces if making individual hotpots).

Arrange the potatoes over the meat in overlapping layers, seasoning each layer. Dot the top layer of potato with the remainder of the butter.

Cover the dish and place on the top shelf of the oven for 2 hours. Uncover and cook for a further 30 minutes. If the potatoes are not brown by this point, turn up the oven and cook for a further 15 minutes, or finish off under the grill, brushing the potato slices with more butter if they look too dry.

BETTY'S HOTPOT IS AS FAMOUS AS THE ROVERS RETURN. SERVED WITH CHIPS AND RED CABBAGE IT COMPLEMENTS NEWTON & RIDLEY'S BEST MILD AND BITTER.

FOR THE LOVE OF RAQUEL

"Not since Mrs Thatcher in her prime has there been a woman so uncrushable, unshakeable and utterly unperturbed by what goes on around her as Coronation Street's *Raquel Wolstenhulme."*

THE NEWS OF THE WORLD, January 1993

RAQUEL WOLSTENHULME moved from Bettabuy supermarket to the bar of The Rovers Return in January 1992. She had returned to the area after a disastrous attempt at modelling and was taken on at the pub by Alec Gilroy, despite Bet's doubts about her abilities: "She's useless! Alec thinks a pretty face can do no wrong. If Miss Marshmallow Brains Wolstenhulme came in here and connected the barrels to the cistern so the toilets were flushing best bitter, he'd still think it was a good idea."

For actress Sarah Lancashire it was a dream come true: "I was so pleased when I discovered Raquel was going to work in the Rovers. Nobody mentions *Coronation Street* without mentioning The Rovers Return and I was just amazed that I was going to be a part of it. I also knew that the possibilities for Raquel would be much greater behind the bar."

Up to this point, Raquel had been seen on screen for only a few months and the character was drastically different: more sober, less flamboyant and more like the actress who plays her. Sarah realised that Raquel could blossom in the Rovers, mixing with a whole range of characters rather than just the supermarket crowd. As well as changing her physical appearance – the dresses became skimpier, the hair more elaborate – Sarah concentrated on altering Raquel's voice, making it higher and more spirited. She also started to play around with Raquel's lines, adding sex appeal to questions such as "What can I get you, Mr Baldwin?" and simpers to "Thank you very much, I don't mind if I do."

When the episodes are screened, approximately three months after the scripts have been written, the writers see new creations for the first time. Sarah used those three months to mould Raquel, basing her loosely on a girl who she had worked with in a wine bar: "The first six months of being in the Rovers became like a tennis match between me and the writers because I knew what I wanted to do with her, I knew what potential she had and the writers started to pick up on it."

Sarah Lancashire is as different from Raquel as Betty Driver is similar to Betty Turpin. Before the make-up artists set to work, Sarah arrives in jeans and floppy jumpers, her long hair hanging straight – so unlike Raquel's baroque styles. Off screen, she is besotted with her young sons, Thomas and Matthew, and spends most of her spare time in her garden.

Sarah had grown up with *Coronation Street*, as her father, Geoffrey Lancashire, spent seven

"I'M NOT A COMPLICATED PERSON." RAQUEL HAS ALWAYS ENJOYED THE SIMPLE THINGS IN LIFE AND GETS UPSET WHEN PEOPLE TREAT HER LIKE AN IDIOT.

years as a regular Street writer, penning 74 episodes, including Episode 569, in which Bet Lynch first appeared. Sarah made her own first appearance in the programme in 1987, when she played nurse Wendy Farmer who answered an advertisement to lodge with the Duckworths at No. 9. Jack, predictably, was all for having her but Vera refused, saying the room was just right for her mother.

Growing up in Oldham, Lancashire, Sarah had no ambition to be an actress; she was much more interested in writing. However, the acting bug hit her at school and she went on to the Guildhall School of Drama. She sang with a dance band for six years and lectured in theatre studies between acting roles. Sarah enjoys playing Raquel, although she isn't always happy about the way she is categorised as a dumb blonde: "It's a constant battle being blonde because of this awful bimbo thing. I don't know who invented the word, but it has made it really boring to be blonde."

On screen, Angie Freeman stuck a dagger deep into Raquel's heart when she delighted in telling her she was a bimbo. The bitchiness between Angie and Raquel (it started when Raquel stole Des from Angie) was a great treat for Sarah to play: "I do find it hard to like her [Raquel] when she's being bitchy – but it is really because she wants to be adored and told how much she is loved. The trouble is, she really isn't bright enough to be bitchy."

JACK'S GLASSES

A Mystery Resolved

"Jack's rather an unpleasant type. He's quite happy with his pie and a pint, and just leaves Vera to it."

WILLIAM TARMEY

JACK DUCKWORTH first appeared in *Coronation Street* in November 1979, when he was a guest at Brian and Gail Tilsley's wedding. He disgraced himself at the reception, getting drunk and leaving for The Legion to avoid taking his wife Vera home. It was to be another six years before Jack pulled his first pint.

However, Bill Tarmey, the actor who plays Jack, first appeared behind the Rovers' bar in 1978! The episode centred on another marriage - that of Alf Roberts and Renee Bradshaw. Alf's friends Annie and Bet were invited to the reception in the Select, so a man was sent from the brewery to help Betty out behind the bar. The man had no name and never spoke, and was played by Bill Tarmey.

Born in a Manchester back-street, Bill worked in the building trade and at one time ran a shop before turning his sights to show-business. He worked the local clubs as a singer and spent his days acting as an extra at Granada. In the memorable television production of King Lear with Lord Olivier in the title role, Bill donned a beard to serve as a knave. For many years he wandered around in the background as an extra at the Rovers; on one

occasion he had to knock the bar flap down onto Ernie Bishop's hand.

Jack is now firmly established as the Rovers' cellarman, but his time behind the bar has been dogged by ill fortune, dodgy deals, unrequited lusts and the unerring knack of putting his money on the wrong horse.

One memorable storyline revolved around money missing from the till. Bet suspected that one of the staff was stealing but she finally discovered Jack was giving too much change as his eyesight was getting worse. Rather than admit as much, Jack stormed out of the pub, his male pride hurt. He later confessed to Vera that his body was changing: "Me 'air's fallin' out. Me teeth are goin'. I'm not as randy as I was. And I've got athlete's foot." Vera bullied Jack into seeing an optician and he returned to work with a new pair of glasses.

Jack is now renowned for his glasses and the piece of sticking plaster which keeps them from falling apart. Jack refuses to have them mended as he can't afford it and the *Coronation Street* wardrobe department regularly receives spectacles in the post from people concerned about Jack's eyesight.

Bill Tarmey uses Jack's glasses as a wonderful comic device: the sharp-eyed viewer will

often spot him in the background of a scene, searching for them, finding them, trying to adjust them or referring to them gloomily. In fact Bill is to blame for breaking the glasses in the first place. He recalls the incident in 1989 which led Jack to raid the first-aid box: "About a fortnight after Jack was given the glasses, I was sat in my dressing room, between recording scenes. I had been reading with my glasses and was called for the next scene. I stood up and stood on Jack's new glasses. The arm was completely off and I realised I had broken them. I needed them in the next scene so I told Liz [Dawn - who plays Vera] that I would be mending the glasses in that scene. I then went to props and got a roll of plaster. So all the way through the scene, whilst Jack was talking to Vera, instead of doing his racing he sat there putting the plaster on the glasses."

At the age of 51, William Tarmey fulfilled a

ONE SMALL INCIDENT TURNED A PROP INTO A MAJOR TALKING POINT: WILLIAM TARMEY AND THOSE FAMOUS GLASSES.

lifelong ambition when his single "One Voice" hit the music charts. On the record, Bill was backed by the children from St Winifred's Choir. The royalties from the single went to a new charity for underprivileged children, The Aquinas Trust, which was launched by fellow *Coronation Street* star, Helen Worth (Gail Platt). Bill first sang on television on his *This Is Your Life* show in 1992. He sang "Wind Beneath My Wings" to his wife Alma, whom he married when he was 21. Bill is a family man whose spare time is often spent playing with his grandchildren Curtis, Matthew, Naomi and Leigh.

THE QUEENS

New Pub on the Block

*"That's the fastest takeover
I've seen in peace-time."*

BET GILROY

*B*ET GILROY's sense of security was thrown upside down in 1993 when Liz McDonald, a barmaid she had trained up in two years, was given her own pub. To add insult to injury, the pub she took on was the brewery's showpiece, in the heart of Weatherfield with a clientele of professional types. Bet was jealous, Liz was thrilled, but Jim McDonald was suspicious.

Jim felt, as Bet did, that Liz's rise on the Newton & Ridley ladder had been too swift and, his mind fuelled by bitchy gossips, he came to the conclusion that brewery boss Richard Willmore had more in store for Liz that a new pub. Liz was incensed by Jim's suggestion that she had been unfaithful and

LEFT: JIM McDONALD COULD NOT COPE WITH WORKING AS HIS WIFE'S EMPLOYEE. AFTER TWO WEEKS HIS JEALOUSY GOT THE BETTER OF HIM AND HE THUMPED RICHARD WILLMORE IN AN ATTEMPT TO FREE THEM BOTH OF THE PUB. JIM'S PLAN BACKFIRED WHEN LIZ CHOSE THE PUB OVER HIM. HIS PLACE WAS FILLED BY COLIN BARNES (RIGHT) WHO DECIDED HE WANTED JIM'S WIFE AS WELL AS HIS JOB.

accused him of being jealous of her success – it was her name above the door, her pub and he was nothing but a failure. The dream of a new life at The Queens soured during the Summer of 1993 as the McDonald family was ripped apart by Jim's jealousy.

This story was the first time *Coronation Street* had shown two pubs running simultaneously for an extended period. The Flying Horse and such pubs were seen only occasionally and for short-lived stories. The Queens however was seen in nearly every episode from the time it was introduced.

Beverley Callard, the actress who plays Liz, was worried at first that she would feel alienated from the rest of the cast, as all the Queens scenes are recorded on location at a Manchester pub rather than in the studio: "The Queens is incredibly different, first it's much more stressful because it's all shot on PSC (Portable Single Camera); last Sunday we did 16 scenes and you don't have a break whilst they do a Kabin scene or Corner Shop scene, it's all me. And I have to get changed during the tea break, or everyone would be waiting around while I get ready. So I find it quite stressful."

Like many *Coronation Street* stories, this particular one originated from a small problem: Julie Goodyear wanted to take a three-week holiday. The writers realised Bet would also have to go away, otherwise it would look odd if she was continuously absent from the Rovers. The decision was made that Bet and Rita would go on holiday together to Tenerife, leaving Bet with the problem of finding someone to run the pub. Producer Carolyn Reynolds takes up the story: "Really Liz was the only choice. Jack had gone before and didn't get it. Raquel offered, which was a lovely moment because we had Bet turning her down, and the conflict that that caused between Liz and Raquel. You had Betty saying she didn't want the responsibility."

In the past, whenever the landlord or landlady was absent, things at the Rovers ground to a halt. Annie Walker was always returning from a visit to find staff missing, her pub in the local press, money missing, dissatisfied customers and – on one occasion – a whole new regime behind the bar. This time Bet returned home to just the opposite: everything was fine, Liz had done a wonderful job and furthermore had been promised her own pub! This made Bet feel very insecure.

There was never any intention to set The Queens up as a rival for The Rovers Return. The customers are completely different, as is the atmosphere in the pub. "The strength of this is really a McDonald story about their marriage, rather than about pubs," explained Carolyn Reynolds. "The Queens is really a setting in which to see the problems that Liz is going through. It is really more the conflict of that drama rather than the setting of it that's important. You want to get the feeling that the Rovers is some little back-street pub, whereas The Queens is much more city life, it's more central Weatherfield. It's modern, there's a lot of money being spent on it. Maybe it's not as friendly, quite cold."

As to the future of the pub, Carolyn sees no threat to the Rovers: "I don't see any long-term benefit in having two pubs, I think one is enough. The Rovers will always be the main meeting point, the main pub."

As Beverley Callard pointed out, all The Queens scenes are recorded on location. This is unusual as the majority of sets are to be found in the *Coronation Street* studio at Granada Television. The decision to use a real pub was made by the producer: "There's a certain feel to our location filming, maybe it's a grainier quality or more atmospheric. Technically the location camera is better and you've got better lighting. I felt that the visual impact would be far greater if you went out to a new location and used that. You feel a distance between the Rovers and The Queens then, and that is what I wanted to create. A difference. You feel as though you are away from the Street when you see The Queens which was the idea; it's a pub away from Coronation Street."

The History Of
THE QUEENS

The Queens was originally built in 1931 and named "The Queen's Arms" to commemorate the exiled Henrietta Maria, the wife of Charles I, who had attempted to raise an army to help her husband. The French queen lived from 1609 to1669 and was the mother of Charles II. The pub sign over the main pub entrance is taken from a painting, from which the sculptor Bernini was to create a bust.

FAMOUS FACES

"Bet, can I have a word wi' your leader. Not Margaret Thatcher, the other one - Annie 'Get Yer Gun' Walker."

RAY LANGTON

ELSIE TANNER:
"What do you think of Margaret Thatcher?"
ENA SHARPLES:
"She's happily married which is more than you are."

BRITAIN'S FIRST female Prime Minister, Margaret Thatcher, had been the butt of the Coronation Street residents' jokes since 1975, not so much for her politics, but because Annie Walker modelled herself on her. Mrs Thatcher actually visited the Street, and the pub, in February 1990. The event was televised by the news teams and the entire cast were to be present in the pub for her entrance. Unfortunately, the premier was running late and it was feared that she would have no time to visit the pub set. The actors were well rehearsed for the expected entrance, with Julie Goodyear, in character as Bet, standing behind the bar to welcome the visitor in good old *Coronation Street* fashion – with a glass of champagne and a plate of Betty's hotpot. However, in the event Julie never managed to deliver the planned welcome as Mrs Thatcher arrived at top speed and delighted the cast by recognising each one of them. Turning to Julie, she beamed and said: "I understand we have a lot in common – I have a Newton and a Ridley in my cabinet!"

Mrs Thatcher was not the only Prime Minister to enjoy watching *Coronation Street:* Harold Wilson was reported to end his Cabinet meetings promptly on Mondays and Wednesdays so he could catch the programme. In 1966, Doris Speed, Arthur Leslie, and Pat Phoenix (Elsie Tanner) visited Sir Harold at No.10 Downing Street prior to their tour of Australia.

When Her Majesty the Queen opened the new *Coronation Street* set in May 1982 the first actors she met were those standing outside the Rovers. She was introduced to Doris Speed, Betty Driver, Julie Goodyear and Fred Feast and commented on Julie's earrings which sported photographs of the Prince and Princess of Wales. As she moved along the Street, Prince Philip met the cast behind her. Upon meeting Eileen Derbyshire (Emily Bishop), he enquired as to the structure of the Street. Alarming the security men, Miss Derbyshire led the Prince into her "house" to show him its wooden construction.

Over the years, many international stars have broken off tours for the chance to visit the *Coronation Street* set. Most of them, such as Alfred Hitchcock in 1962, have given up a chance to walk down the Street, preferring to pose for their own snap shots in the Rovers, sampling Newton & Ridley's best.

ABOVE: AS A CHILD, MARGARET THATCHER HAD GROWN UP OVER MR ROBERTS' CORNER SHOP. SHE POPPED INTO ALF ROBERTS' SHOP JUST BEFORE SHE VISITED THE ROVERS IN 1990.

RIGHT: DORIS SPEED'S PROUDEST MOMENT CAME IN 1982 WHEN THE QUEEN PAUSED TO CHAT TO HER OUTSIDE THE ROVERS.

LEFT: SHOWING OFF HER PINT-PULLING - ACTRESS DIANA DORS WAS A WELCOME RECRUIT TO ANNIE'S TEAM.

ABOVE: ONE OF HOLLYWOOD'S FINEST MEETS ONE OF ENGLAND'S GREATEST - DUSTIN HOFFMAN CHATS TO PAT PHOENIX DURING A *CORONATION STREET* VISIT.

LEFT: ENA SHARPLES GIVES HELEN SHAPIRO ADVICE ON REACHING TOP NOTES DURING A VISIT IN 1962.

ABOVE: FAMILIAR CHARACTERS TURNED UP IN 1977 TO AUDITION FOR THE ROLES OF ANNIE'S NEW BAR STAFF. SHE THOUGHT MICKEY, PLUTO AND GOOFY MIGHT BE AN IMPROVEMENT ON FRED, BET AND BETTY.

RIGHT: BY 1961 THE ROVERS RETURN WAS SO FAMOUS THAT INTERNATIONAL STARS SUCH AS ALFRED HITCHCOCK COULDN'T RESIST POPPING IN WHEN THEY WERE IN THE AREA.

TALES FROM THE ROVERS

"The things that have gone on in this pub!
If only walls could talk."

BETTY TURPIN

1961

FRESH FROM TEACHER-TRAINING COLLEGE, Joan Walker was successful in her first job interview. She started work at a primary school in Derby in September 1960 and by Christmas was engaged to fellow teacher Gordon Davies. The wedding, planned for the following March, sent Joan's mother Annie into a spin; three months was such short notice to get everything organised properly – there were invitations to send, the reception to book, dresses to buy and, most importantly, Gordon's shopkeeping parents to impress.

In the middle of all the preparations, Annie's 18-year-old son Billy returned from completing his National Service and for a couple of weeks Annie had to contend with worries about whether or not he would settle down. Whereas Joan had always been reliable, studious and sensible, Billy had rebelled and fought his way through life. With the Davies coming to high tea Annie worried that Billy's coarseness could ruin his sister's chance of marrying into the socially acceptable family.

Jack Walker, accustomed to his wife's social ambitions, tried his best to defuse the situa-

tion, but his down-to-earth "I believe in taking people as you find them" attitude exasperated Annie. As far as she was concerned, one had to be seen to be respectable at all times. Therefore it was a necessity that the Stuart Crystal was on display, the table was covered with fine Irish linen and that Jack and Billy wore ties.

Joan was as anxious as her mother that the Walker men should not let her down in any way. She was horrified when Billy arrived for the meal dressed to kill: "It's a smasher isn't it? Italian style you know. Fourteen inch bottoms and no turn ups. Cost me fourteen quid but I thought it would come in for the wedding." Siding with her daughter, Annie ordered Billy upstairs to change. Didn't he understand that sharp Italian suits were not to be worn in polite company?

Despite Annie's attempts to impress, the first meeting with Hilda and George Davies did not go as planned. Gordon's mother took every opportunity to make sure her hostess realised she was marrying into class: "I was married in white myself. White satin, with a lace veil. My mother cried all the way to the church. Three bridesmaids I had. All in pink,

1961 GIVEN THE CHANCE OF A NEW
PUB, THE ROYAL OAK, THE WALKERS
BOTH DECIDED THEY WERE TOO OLD.

and a child attendant in mari-
bou". Whilst Annie battled to
get a word in with the over-
bearing Hilda, Jack enticed
teetotal George to view his
cellar. Unfortunately, the
best bitter barrel slipped
and burst all over George's
new suit. Whilst publicly
berating Jack for his clumsi-
ness, Annie secretly
delighted in Hilda's mortified expression.

The residents of Coronation Street stood in
their doorways on the morning of 8 March
1961 as Jack proudly walked his daughter out
of the pub and into the waiting car. Pensioners
Ena Sharples and Martha Longhurst watched
the family guests leaving for the church from
plum positions outside the pub. Ena tried to
work out how much it was all costing: "That's
four cars I've counted, an' I think I missed
one while I was puttin' me coat on to come
out. It must be costin' Jack Walker a bob or
two this lot. Still, if they can't afford it, who
can?" Her neighbour Martha was not so charitable: "There's nobody outside the family bin
invited you know. 'E could 'ave asked one or
two of the regulars. After the money we've
spent, a free meal at the reception wouldn't
'ave cost 'im so much. Not that it's 'im, it's
her."

A chance to better themselves came the
Walkers' way in the Autumn of 1961. The couple had spent two weeks holidaying in
Torquay, having left the running of the pub in
the hands of relief manager Vince Plummer.
Cockney Vince criticised the way the Walkers
ran the pub and wrote to the brewery with his
recommendations about how the Rovers should
be run. The Walkers ner-
vously awaited a visit from the brewery, but
when it came they were stunned. The brewery
Rep Mr Lloyd came not to investigate
Plummer's accusations but to offer the Walkers
the chance to run the brewery's latest show
pub: "It's called The Royal Oak. An' it's a
beauty Mrs Walker. Car park, five rooms, cock-
tail bar, fitted carpets. All modern an' bang up
to date. You must admit it's a bit different from
The Rovers Return. Different sort o' clientele
altogether. Not like some of the ruffians you
get round 'ere."

Thrilled at the thought of cocktails and
cloakrooms, Annie splashed out on a new hat
and corset to ensure she looked the part when
she viewed the pub. Although she looked right,
Annie wasn't sure if she felt right: "It's worse
than breaking in new shoes. Why did that fitter
woman smell of peppermints? Y'know, before I
even as much as 'ad time to offer 'er a drink
she was gazing longingly at me liqueur bottles.
I don't think 'er mind was on controllin' my figure at all. I think it was working overtime on
me Cherry Brandy."

With the new hat, but without the offending corset, Annie and Jack eagerly looked over The Royal Oak. It was indeed beautiful, spacious and luxurious but Annie wasn't sure if its new fittings would stand up to much handling: "Why leatherette walls Mr Lloyd? Have you ever presented the drinkin' public with a different sort of plain new wall? It's asking for trouble. There's nothing they like better than adulterating a novelty surface."

Jack was pleased to see Annie's obvious joy in the new pub. He was willing enough to take on the Oak for her sake, although he would be sad to leave behind all his regulars, who were friends rather than customers. However, he knew the move would be important to Annie and had no wish to hold her back. If she wanted a fridge that was big enough to walk into then she should have it; she deserved the best. His only worry was that he was too old to start again and he confided in his friends, telling them his true feelings: "These new-fangled places, with their chromium fittin's and mod. cons. in every corner – they need young 'uns with a bit of go in 'em. It's fer Annie's sake I'm goin' – not mine. She's 'ad a tough time 'ere and she deserves summat better."

Ironically, Annie was thinking the same as Jack. She realised the new pub would be hard to run and, like Jack, felt too old to adjust. When she asked him outright if he wanted to move, Jack hesitated long enough for Annie to realise he did not. Counting their blessings they decided to stay exactly where they were.

1962

CONCEPTA HEWITT (NEE RILEY) had lived with the Walkers for two years. In that time she and Annie became the best of friends: Concepta admired and tried to copy Annie's tastes and views whilst Annie found the younger woman charming in her willingness to help. Her husband Harry was one of the Rovers' best customers and a good friend to Jack, occasionally helping him out behind the bar. However, an incident in January 1962 threatened their friendship for a few days, and alienated Annie from the rest of the Street.

Cashing up at the end of a hard day, Annie was puzzled to find the till was £20 short. Her mind quickly recalled that Dennis Tanner, who

1962 JACK WAS THE ONLY PERSON LEFT IN THE PUB TO CONSOLE ANNIE WHEN SHE FOUND THE MISSING MONEY - EVERYONE ELSE HAD BEEN DRIVEN AWAY.

had once been imprisoned for petty thieving, had been alone in the pub for a few minutes earlier in the evening. Annie immediately decided that the disappearance must have had something to do with him: "I'm the last one to want to cause any unpleasantness. But I'm not going to be made a fool of. Specially by the Tanners."

When Dennis next came into the pub he was stunned when Annie curtly told him that his custom was no longer welcome. Dennis' mother Elsie was furious to discover that Annie suspected Dennis of theft; she knew her son well enough to know he would never steal from his own doorstep. Annie was dismayed and embarrassed when, in front of a pub full of customers, Elsie produced Ena Sharples as a witness to the fact that Dennis had not touched the till; she had been in the Snug all the time. Annie knew that Mission caretaker Ena was telling the truth and was lost for words. Elsie, however wasn't: "I'm not goin' to ask for an apology like certain people, Mrs Annie Walker! I'm goin' now an' I won't be comin' back."

Elsie led a boycott of The Rovers Return which quickly spread as Annie, refusing to admit she was in the wrong, stuck to her notion that if Dennis had not stolen the money someone else had. One by one she turned on her customers, casting doubt upon their honesty. Jack watched helplessly as the regulars left in droves: "You know what I think Annie. An' you know I'll back you up an' all. I'm not sticking up for you because I think you're right. You're me wife an' that's good enough. Short of lockin' you up in t' W.C. there's not much else I can do. But just don't think I'm enjoyin' it. That's all."

Eventually Annie turned her suspicions upon Harry Hewitt. Concepta was furious that her husband was insulted and walked out on the Walkers. Annie genuinely did not understand why she had left: "I never thought the day would come when Concepta turned against me. She's been more like a daughter to me, that girl."

After suffering three days of standing behind a bar in a deserted pub, Annie broke down. Confused, and feeling that she was – had to be – in the right, she confessed to Jack that she did not know what she had to do. Someone must have taken the £20, mustn't they? It was not a joyful occasion for Annie when, polishing the offending till that night, she found four five-pound notes caught behind the till drawer. Annie retired to her bed, and understanding Jack took the weight of the situation upon his shoulders, apologising to the regulars and telling them he had lost and found the money. Slowly the rovers returned.

1963

A BOTTLE OF SHERRY caused problems for the Walkers in the Spring of 1963. Jack had bought some bottles of cheap sherry from local petty criminal Jed Stone. He had stored them in the cellar, planning to use them whenever Annie's living-room decanter needed refilling. Unfortunately, he forgot to inform Annie and, alone behind the bar one evening, she opened a bottle to serve a customer. The person she served it to turned out to be Mr Henshaw, a brewery representative. He coldly reminded Annie that it was against brewery rules to sell sherry not supplied by Newton & Ridley. Taking the bottle as evidence, he told her of his intention to report the Walkers. Worried that the licence could be in jeopardy, Annie blamed everything on Jack: "How would I know that you would be stupid enough to buy bootleg sherry. I mean, you stayed loyal to the brewery even when the Americans were offerin' you that cheap whisky...."

Jack was summoned to the brewery to explain the matter to area manager Fred Hamilton, an old friend of his from the Licensed Victuallers. Annie prepared herself for the worst, but begged Jack to keep his self respect and not to humble himself even though he was afraid of losing the roof over their heads.

Jack was certain he could explain the situation to his old pal Fred and was stung when Hamilton launched into an attack. The area manager told Jack that the brewery had been soft for long enough and would not tolerate the sale of outside stock; they were going to make an example of him

Whilst Jack anxiously tried to make his excuses, Fred burst into laughter, delighted that Jack had fallen for his joke. He apologised for pulling his leg but had not been able to resist the opportunity. Jack was relieved that his integrity was not in question but annoyed that he had been summoned to "the boss" just for a joke.

A couple of months later Annie uncovered treachery amongst her regulars. She found schoolgirl Lucille Hewitt reading some old newspaper cuttings supplied by Ena Sharples. Her blood ran cold when she noticed that one of the cuttings was about a certain Miss A. Beaumont who had ridden down the streets of Weatherfield as Lady Godiva. Annie was horrified because she was the Miss Beaumont in question. She was quick to reassure Jack that the episode had not been improper: "Just for the record, I was covered from head to foot – no, let's be accurate, from my neck to my ankles – in flesh-pink stockinette and I had an unusually long blonde wig."

Annie decided that Ena

must have kept the cutting for blackmail purposes and confronted her, quietly, in the Snug. Ena was indignant when Annie implied she had been looking upon the cutting as an investment. To Annie's horror, Ena's voice rose and carried around the full pub as she retorted: "Even in yer nasty mindedness you try to raise the tone, don't you? Eh, for the good of yer 'ealths I think you lot ought to know that I'm a blackmailer. And Mrs Annie Walker, if you didn't want to be known as Lady Godiva, you shouldn't 'ave flaunted yourself in your nakedness in t'first place!" Anyone who missed the outburst, and Annie's hasty exit into the living room, had the whole tale retold to them that Christmas Day. The residents gathered at the Mission Hall knowing that Dennis Tanner had planned to embarrass one of them with an impromptu "This Is Your Life", but they didn't know was who was to be his victim until he waved his red book in Annie's direction and invited her to mount the stage. She was mortified and rounded upon Jack for not warning her.

1963 DENNIS TANNER PRESENTED A SPECIAL TRIBUTE TO ANNIE WALKER. SHE DELIGHTED IN HAVING THE FAMILY TOGETHER BUT WASN'T AMUSED BY THE REFERENCES TO LADY GODIVA.

For the next half an hour Annie suffered mixed emotions – delight in seeing Joan and Billy again and horror to hear the croaky-voiced milkman who had led the nag when she played the fair Lady. The milkman came onto the stage, cap in hand, to tell all Annie's regulars about that fateful day: "I remember losin' t'procession three times! I mean if you're leadin' an 'orse wi' a naked woman on it, you're not goin' to spend much time lookin' where you're goin', are you?" The Mission Hall resounded with laughter as Annie shifted uncomfortably in her chair.

1964

THE WALKERS employed two members of the same family in 1964 – barmaid Irma Ogden and her mother Hilda, the cleaning lady. Little did Annie suspect that Hilda would survive her at the pub and would clean the bar-top for 23 years! However, both Irma and Hilda's time at the Rovers was very nearly cut short just months after they started.

Irma's 14-year-old brother Trevor often played truant in his bid to become a millionaire before his 21st birthday. He was well known in the markets as a wheeler dealer, stashing away his ill-gotten gains under his mattress. In the Summer of 1964 he managed to buy twelve bags of onions cheap. His only problem was where to store them until a buyer could be found. Roping in Irma – on the promise of a leather jacket – and Mrs Sharples – promising her ten per cent of the profits – Trevor arranged to store the sacks in the Rovers' cellar. Ena kept Annie occupied whilst Irma opened the trap-door to the cellar and stacked the sacks when Trevor had sent them shooting down the barrel chute.

The next day, Trevor found his buyer and had to rope Hilda into the scheme to remove the onions behind Annie's back. Just as Trevor brought up the seventh sack, Annie returned,

1964 SCHOOLGIRL LUCILLE HEWITT ENJOYED MORE FREEDOM AT THE ROVERS THAN SHE HAD UNDER FATHER, HARRY; SO MUCH SO THAT WHEN HER SCHOOLING FINISHED SHE DECIDED TO STAY ON WITH AUNTIE ANNIE.

catching both Trevor and Hilda red-handed.

When the situation was explained she was horrified: "I can assure you, Mrs Ogden, that the condition of a beer cellar is one of the most important aspects of our profession. You and your son have jeopardised our entire future."

Hilda looked suitably chastened, but when Annie started threatening Trevor with a good hiding, Hilda's humility turned to anger. She sided with Trevor, antagonising Annie and prompting further spleen: "There's nothing simple about being deceitful, dishonest and destructive. The boy's a vandal, he's been nothing but a nuisance since he came here." Annie then dismissed Hilda and Irma. Hilda marched out of the pub: "That suits me fine, you jumped-up old bat!" Fortunately for the Ogdens, who needed the money, Jack Walker saw the funny side and reinstated them both.

In the Autumn of 1964, 15-year-old Lucille Hewitt moved into the pub, when her parents went to live in Ireland. to avoid disrupting her education, The Hewitt's close friends the Walkers agreed to take little Lucille on and act as her ward in their absence. What they thought would be a temporary situation actually lasted for ten years, during which time Lucille would become closer to the Walkers than their own daughter ever had been.

1965 THE STRESS OF BEING BLACKMAILED BY TURNER CAUSED JACK TO SUFFER A BREAKDOWN. THE RESIDENTS WERE INCENSED THAT THEIR FRIEND HAD BEEN SO COMPROMISED AND MANY SWORE TO AVENGE HIM. IN THE END IT WAS JERRY BOOTH WHO ASSAULTED TURNER AND SAW HIM OFF FOR GOOD.

1965

"THE LADIES' COMMITTEE is a position of responsibility in the community. Believe me, if the Lady Victuallers disagree with national policy, we take firm action. We're watching NATO, very closely. Oh yes." To Annie Walker, the Weatherfield branch of the Licensed Victuallers Association (Ladies Section) was the United Nations, the Church of England and London society all rolled into one. In 1965, she started her own campaign to be elected chairwoman of the committee for that year. Jack resigned himself to either sitting through twelve months of speeches or having to console Annie throughout the year if she wasn't elected.

Annie relied upon the support of Nellie Harvey, a leading light in the Committee, and to this end invited her for tea, warning Jack to be on his best behaviour. Unfortunately for Annie, Nellie arrived a mite early and caught Annie in her dressing gown and curlers. Nellie did not seem to mind as she was left with "Jackie" for entertainment. Jack did Annie proud, turning on the charm with the flirtatious Nellie. At the end of the evening, Annie was ecstatic when Nellie announced her intention to support her all the way. Annie, aware of her own shortcomings, was under no illusion as to why Nellie was being her champion: "If it hadn't been for you Jack, love, I'd be a nobody today – let alone the Chairman – Elect. It's opened my eyes today. You're wasted on me, Jack Walker. I'm unworthy of you."

Jack found himself in a very delicate situation in December. The Walkers had attended a local wedding, leaving Jack's brother Arthur in charge. He had to leave the bar unattended for a short time, so 16-year-old Lucille kept an eye on the till for him. Frank Turner, an unpleasant stranger, called at the pub and refused to wait for Arthur's return. Lucille felt obliged to serve him and fell into conversation with him. When Jack returned, Turner told him he had no intention of paying for the drinks he'd drunk; Lucille was underage and unless Jack gave him more rum, the brewery would be informed. For the next few weeks, Turner blackmailed Jack for drinks and cigarettes, never paying for them and making sure Jack knew he'd lose his licence if the brewery found out about Lucille serving. Annie was alerted to what was going on and worried for Jack's health as Turner started extorting money from him. Jack suffered a breakdown and collapsed behind the bar. In her distress, Annie blurted out the whole story to the regulars and that evening Turner was viciously beaten up in the Street. The residents evoked their own justice without the brewery or the police finding out anything.

1966

THE REMOVAL OF AN OLD GIRDER in the Rovers' cellar led to an exciting discovery for Annie in the late Spring of 1966. There, behind a lot of rubble and rotten crates, stood a framed oil painting of an aristocratic woman. Jack planned to throw the painting away with the crates but Annie asked an antiques expert his opinion. During his investigation of the piece, he took the frame off and found a mask and some money stashed behind the painting. Annie's romanticised imagination ran overtime and she became intrigued by the mysterious woman: "My theory is that some aristocratic nobleman catching the stage-coach to York – I'm not definitely saying it was Beau Brummel – stayed the night on this site. And probably what happened was he chanced to meet this great lady with her alabaster skin, at a masked ball. Then the Roundheads or suchlike were probably hiding in a secret catacomb..."

1966 ANNIE SOUGHT THE HELP OF TEACHER KEN BARLOW IN TRACING THE ORIGINS OF THE MASKED LADY. BY THE END OF THE WEEK, KEN WAS AS TIRED AS EVERYONE ELSE OF HEARING ANNIE'S ROMANTIC SPECULATIONS.

The regulars soon bored of Annie's stories of dashing noblemen but their lack of interest soon turned to alarm when Annie announced that she intended to change the name of the pub and set up as a tourist attraction. Ena led the fight against "The Masked Lady": "What you're really after is a posh pub, i'nt'it? Like they get Cheshire way. With a bit o' romance be'ind it, an' every oak beam 'as a tale to tell. Well, for cryin' out loud, pack your bags, get on a tram an' move to one! An' give us all a bit of peace."

The brewery considered the idea of changing the Rovers' name when Annie wrote to them saying she had the backing of all the regulars. Jack refused to let Annie offend the regulars by riding rough-shod over their feelings as no one had backed Annie's scheme. He went behind her back to inform the brewery that the regulars liked the pub the way it was.

Annie was disappointed when the brewery decided against a name change. However, her fascination with the enigmatic lady never diminished until the painting disappeared one morning, just after the binmen had been round.

1967

SURPRISINGLY, ANNIE WALKER and her young ward Lucille Hewitt had a very good relationship. Jack was always better at dealing with Lucille's wayward moments, such as when she became a vegetarian or left home to be a hippy, but on day-to-day matters Annie and Lucille existed in a typical mother/daughter relationship. However, Annie had one habit which drove Lucille insane: she opened all the post, regardless of whom it was addressed to. Lucille decided to teach Auntie Annie a lesson, and over a period of weeks Annie was driven to distraction as hundreds of catalogues and brochures, which Lucille had applied for in her name, were delivered to her. The situation became out of control when salesmen arrived to show Annie the wares she had supposedly ordered. Jack found out about the prank and ordered Lucille to stop her games after a salesman tried to sell Annie a motorcycle.

Lucille was amazed when one of the last catalogues – from Cutie-Beauty Cosmetics – was accompanied by a letter addressed to Annie, congratulating her for being the company's 100,000th customer. Her prize was a weekend in Paris with a French film star. Lucille tried to claim the prize as her own, but Annie decided that as the letter was addressed to her, she would go herself. She left for the airport in a chauffeur-driven limousine.

1967 JACK DELIGHTED IN ANNIE'S COME-UPPANCE WHEN THE MENFOLK ORDERED THEIR PINTS IN WINE GLASSES. SHE WAS HURT BY THE TEASING AS SHE HAD ONLY WANTED TO RAISE THE TONE OF THE PUB.

1968 EMILY NUGENT MANAGED TO TAME THE BUILDERS BY REFUSING TO SERVE UNTIL THEY BEHAVED.

Jack and Lucille had to suffer in silence when, on the Monday, Annie returned, her life completely changed after 48 hours on French soil: "Wandering over a Seine bridge in the moonlight, doesn't encourage one to think of *chez moi* or even of one's life partner." If her family had to live with the new Annie, the regulars didn't. They were put off their beer by the sound of Marcosignori's "Musetta Waltz" bellowing from Annie's record player whilst the smell of *lapin rôti* tempted their noses. Jack was long suffering: "It's roast rabbit. Used to turn her stomach but now she can call it *lapin*."

The regulars felt sorry for Jack, although many, like Irma Barlow, enjoyed poking fun at the landlady: "I'm waiting for her to do a can-can."

Jack despaired when Annie announced her plan to put tables and chairs outside on the pavement to create a café atmosphere. He appealed to the regulars for help and, led by Ken Barlow, they set about teaching Annie a lesson. Telling her that wine glasses were more refined than pint pots, the menfolk ordered their bitter and mild in wine glasses, downing the contents in one and asking for more immediately, calculating that 5 wine glasses equalled one pint. Annie tried to leave the bar rather than be mocked by her customers, but Jack stopped her: "I'm sick of hearing about Paris and so is everybody else. Now I ask you love – is it worth it, eh?" With her lip trembling, Annie made a dignified exit and Paris was never mentioned again in the bar.

1968

SPINSTER EMILY NUGENT was the sort of person Annie could relate to: genteel, quiet, educated and refined. When Emily was made homeless in April 1968, Annie told her that Joan's room was vacant and ready for her. Rather than inviting her to move in as a paying guest, she asked Emily when she would be ready to move in, giving her no choice in the matter – Annie had chosen her to be her companion. Emily put in the plea that a public house was not her sort of place: "I've just never seen myself sleeping a rafter away from a public bar. They still tend to be rudely male, don't they?" But Annie's mind was made up: "Hardly a public house Miss Nugent. More a hotel. Who knows, I might eventually aspire to the AA Guide."

Emily moved her suitcases in, agreeing with Annie that the folk-weave curtains were a joy to look at. Unfortunately, no sooner had she unpacked her vanity case than she was called to the bar by Jack. He explained that Annie and

Lucille were in bed ill with a bug and he was feeling liverish. Pushing Emily into the Public Bar, Jack assured her she'd cope admirably. Emily protested: "Of course, Mr Walker, I was brought up in haberdashery..." but she found herself alone behind the bar, with a crowd of thirsty workmen on the other side of it, waiting to be served: "What do you know lads. Meet the new barmaid. We're going to have a wild night tonight."

The customers soon started to mess Emily about, trying to muddle her over orders and change. She did her best to cope alone but became frightened when some of the men became aggressive; she gave them ready-salted crisps when they wanted plain with a bag of salt. Emily surprised the men by turning on them and, just as Jack thought she was capable of doing, taking control of the situation: "The next gentleman to pinch my bottom will be struck right on his big, red, boozer's nose. I'm withdrawing my labour." Emily sat at one of the tables, refusing to serve until the men behaved like gentlemen. The builders were shocked into complying. Annie was amazed at

the way she had tamed the hoards, so Emily let her into her secret: "Tact, diplomacy, blackmail – nothing to it. For every two pints, I tell them a joke. That keeps them sweet."

Emily was to remain in the Rovers – and occasionally behind the bar – until 1972, when she left the pub to marry Ernest Bishop and to set up home at No. 3, where she still lives with lodger Percy Sugden.

1969

NEWTON & RIDLEY ran a one-off competition in 1969 to find their most popular landlady, putting up a holiday for two in Majorca as first prize. Annie decided that the brewery might as well forget the competition and just give her the plane tickets, but realising that formalities had to be observed, she set about winning her customers over, telling them it was a pleasure and privilege to serve them. To humour her, Ray Langton nominated her for the competition, realising just how much it was costing her to be polite to everyone: "If she tries any 'arder she's goin' to break somethin'."

Jack could not believe it when Sir Ridley sent a telegram congratulating Annie on winning the competition. Jack and Lucille tried to dodge the radiant Annie, but she followed them around the pub, reading her glowing letter from the brewery.

1969 TO JACK'S SURPRISE, ANNIE WON THE "PERFECT LANDLADY" COMPETITION. SHE LATER FRAMED THE TELEGRAM AND HUNG IT IN THE BAR.

Jack upset Annie by refusing to go to Majorca with her as he was afraid of flying. To spite Jack, Annie offered to take Ena instead, expecting her to decline, and was perturbed when she accepted the offer. Jack choked back a smile at the thought of the unlikely pair as Annie and Ena flew out of the country together to spend the next two weeks in each other's company.

Ena returned to the Street alone. She confided to Emily that Annie had spent all her time with a strange man and had decided to stay on with him, giving Ena a letter explaining the situation to Jack. Emily agreed with Ena that the letter must be a "Dear John" and that if Jack did not receive it then he would worry about Annie, fly out to her and that they would be reconciled.

Whilst Jack pondered Annie's absence, Ena and Emily kept quiet. A week later they felt they had done the right thing when Annie returned to the pub. However, she wasn't seeking a reconciliation as none was needed: the mysterious man had been Douglas Cresswell from the brewery and the letter had contained instructions for Jack to contact her urgently – they had been offered the chance to run the brewery's latest pub, in Majorca.

Emily and Ena were both horrified when they learnt the truth. Emily offered to move out of the Rovers whilst Ena blamed Annie for acting suspiciously. Jack, realising the new pub was the answer to all Annie's dreams, agreed to emigrate and Lucille was delighted to find that the offer extended to her as well.

At the last minute, the brewery withdrew the offer, telling the disappointed Walkers that Jack was considered too old to run the new pub. Annie put on a brave face and turned the leaving party into a party to celebrate the fact that they were staying.

A few months later, in June of 1970, Annie would look back at the opportunity and thank God they had not been accepted by the brewery. The Walkers celebrated the new decade along with the other regulars, unaware that Jack had only months to live.

1970

THE SUDDEN DEATH OF JACK WALKER stunned the Street's residents. He had been holidaying at his daughter Joan's house in Derby when he suffered a fatal heart attack. After his funeral in Derby, Annie returned to the Rovers with her son Billy. She was quick to reassure anxious customers that the pub would still have a Walker at the helm – herself. Billy moved in to help run the pub along with Lucille, Emily and new barmaid Betty Turpin.

Tired of her years behind the bar, Annie decided to adopt the role of hostess, imagining herself mingling with the clientele, cocktail in hand. Her plans suffered a blow when Emily announced that she could no longer help out behind the bar as it reflected badly upon her growing relationship with lay-preacher Ernest Bishop.

Despondent, Annie resigned herself to having to struggle on but the next day Billy announced that he had hired the perfect barmaid – brassy and bold Bet Lynch, manageress of the local launderette.

Annie returned from a shopping trip to find Bet, in a tight black dress, pulling her first pint as the local men leered at her. Sniffing at Bet as she passed, Annie walked straight into the living room with Billy tagging on behind. As she pulled at her gloves, Annie launched into an attack: "Would you mind telling Miss Lynch to get dressed and go home, and then perhaps you'll be kind enough to tell me what she's doing behind my bar...I will not have the standard of this pub lowered to something more suitable for the dock road!" Billy pleaded for Bet to stay, adamant that Bet would pull in the customers. Annie agreed to give her a week's trial and was amazed, at the end of that first week, that Billy was right about the girl; she was an asset and she would be a fool to get rid of her. Twenty-three years later Bet is still the main attraction at the pub.

Betty Turpin had ruled the roost behind the

1970 WITH THE SUPPORT OF BET AND BETTY, ANNIE FACED THE FUTURE AS A WIDOW. THEIR FIRST TASK WAS TO DECORATE THE ROVERS' LIVING ROOM.

bar before Bet's appearance and she felt very put out by all the fuss created by the new barmaid: "She's got blonde hair, dangly earrings and neckline right down to 'er ankles." She complained bitterly when Annie gave Bet time off over Christmas and Annie realised that she needed to meet Betty half way to stop her walking out. She decided to flatter Betty: "You and Bet Lynch share the same Christian name and that could lead to friction. I was wondering if you'd mind if from now on I called Bet 'Bet', and referred to you by your full name of Elizabeth." Betty was confused by the conversation and could not see what difference it made, but Annie won her round: "There's a world of difference between a full name and its diminutive. Take your name for instance – Elizabeth. In its full flower – immediately evocative, I always think, of all that is finest in our English heritage. Whereas Bet – don't you think it's just a little common?" Betty walked away from the conversation very pleased with herself.

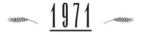

1971

LUCILLE HEWITT started a new career in the early 1970s – that of layabout. Annie took Lucille's reluctance to find employment as a personal affront: she had never been idle herself and could not understand Lucille's attitude, especially when Lucille admitted she expected Annie to keep her: "Auntie Annie, there's a smashing coat in Morton's sale. It's plum-coloured, mid-length, with silver buttons all the way down the front. It's only ten quid."

For months Annie tried to hide Lucille's situation from the her customers, not wanting to bring shame on to her house. However, when Lucille kept refusing jobs her dole was stopped, but the girl still refused to buckle down and find employment. Annie's patience ran out and she stunned her ward by hitting back: "Lucille, as you seem totally incapable of finding a job that you don't consider beneath your dignity, there seems to be only one other source of income left open to you. The Ministry of Social Security."

Lucille was horrified: "You can't mean the Assistance! They'd send a bloke round to check if there was anything I could flog. You can't want a man like that coming to the Rovers." Annie, however, was determined to shake Lucille: "The one thing I'm not prepared to do, Lucille, is to subsidise your fecklessness any further."

The thought of someone going through her belongings, telling her to sell her precious record player, prompted Lucille to reconsider her position, just as Annie had intended. That very afternoon Lucille announced she had found a job. Annie was delighted at the turnaround as

Lucille explained why she had to work evenings – she was a receptionist at the YWCA.

Newton & Ridley decided to pick up on the success of the new psychedelic clubs by refurbishing the old Robin Hood pub and turning it into The Aquarius Disco Pub. Landlady Kitty Stonely rose to the occasion, tinted her hair, updated her wardrobe and drifted into the disco scene. Visiting the pub on its first night, Nellie Harvey was stunned by the loud music, flashing nights and nubile dancers parading around on platforms in shorts and bikini tops. Before the evening was out she had made a mental note to return to the pub the next evening – with Annie.

Annie could not understand what all the fuss was about when she visited the Aquarius and the music threatened to bring on a migraine. She was about the leave when the dancers appeared and the unmistakable shape of her young ward go-goed her way along the platform in Annie's direction.

All that night Lucille and Annie rowed about Lucille's new job. Annie ordered Lucille to write a letter of

1972 THE SELECT, CHRISTMAS DAY: RITA LITTLEWOOD BRINGS THE HOUSE DOWN WITH HER RENDITION OF "LILY MARLENE".

1971 LUCILLE PROVIDED NELLIE HARVEY WITH THE ULTIMATE AMMUNITION AGAINST ANNIE WHEN SHE DANCED AT THE AQUARIUS.

resignation but was forced to adopt a more understanding attitude when Lucille humbly complied with her wishes and read her the letter she was planning to send to the brewery: "...Mrs Anne Walker licensee of your public house The Rovers Return, with who I reside, has publicly expressed her hostility to the whole idea of Disco pubs, and has demanded that I leave my employment with you immediately." Not wishing to face the brewery's response to such a letter, Annie swallowed hard and allowed Lucille to run her own life.

1972

"LOOK MAM... what would you say to me taking the licence to this place on?" Billy finally built up his courage to suggest that, at 63, the time had come for Annie to retire. She was surprised by the question and startled when Billy admitted he had been approached by the brewery to take over. Calling her

1973 AFTER 36 YEARS OF SERVING BEHIND THE BAR, ANNIE CONTEMPLATED HER FUTURE AND DECIDED THAT THE TIME HAD COME TO MOVE ON. THE RESIDENTS, HOWEVER, HAD OTHER IDEAS.

only son a Judas, Annie couldn't understand why the brewery would want her out: "Are we down on beerage? Have the regulars strayed away? Have there been complaints from the Police? No."

Annie marched straight round to the brewery offices on Albert Road and, seeking out her old friend Douglas Cresswell, voiced her concern about being forced into retirement. She returned home feeling more secure: "Status quo. The dictionary is there for all to read and enjoy. So is the name above The Rovers Return."

The split between Annie and Billy was healed when Annie realised that the Billy had not wanted her out but had feared she would leave voluntarily and the Walker Empire would end: "I realise you were only concerned with the Walker name. Your father's name."

1973

THE ROVERS RETURN was thrown into chaos early in 1973 when Annie graciously agreed to become the next Mayoress of Weatherfield. Alf Roberts, one of Annie's more socially acceptable customers, had been made Mayor Elect and, when his first choice turned him down, he asked Annie to be his consort for the year. Annie protested momentarily before jumping at the chance. The barstaff looked on in horror as Annie spent days in Cheshire shopping for "little numbers", employed an elocution teacher, "just to help with the speeches, of course," and tried to install in them all the idea that the Rovers should rise, socially, just as she had. She contemplated refusing to allow men into the bar unless they wore ties, but Billy pointed out that everyone would go to The Flying Horse instead.

At first Billy took over as manager while Annie carried out her official duties, but when Annie discovered that he had run up large gambling debts, and had been using the pub cheque book to get himself out of trouble, Alf pointed out that she risked losing the pub if she allowed Billy to compromise her in this way.

Annie transferred the money from her own account and Billy returned to the work he was trained at – as a garage mechanic.

Betty ran the pub for a short while before Glyn Thomas took over. He was one of the brewery's top managers and he introduced a number of innovations, which proved unpopular with the regulars.

Lucille was startled to overhear a conversation in which Annie told the brewery that she intended to give the pub up for good. Not knowing what to do, Lucille confided in Ena Sharples who agreed that Annie's mind would have to be changed for her. Annie refused to discuss the matter with Ena but Mrs Sharples was not to be put off: "If it doesn't concern t'customers who runs this pub, I'd like to know who it does concern."

Spokesperson Ena called a general meeting at the Rovers and Annie wearily listened as the regulars pleaded with her not to let the Rovers be turned into a seedy back-street boozer. Ena set the tone of the meeting: "We've had plenty of rows in the past and I expect we'll have plenty more before we turn our toes up. But if it's a choice between you running this pub and that upstart out there then I'm 'avin' you every time." One by one Annie's friends and neighbours asked her to stay. She was stunned when Ena produced a petition signed by all the regulars pledging their support to her. Her mind was finally made up when the brewery asked her to stay on. Telling the regulars the good news, she announced drinks on the house. Ena Sharples toasted her: "You know Annie Walker, I always reckoned you'd more sense than folk give you credit for!"

1974

LOCAL CORSET MAKER, blousy Blanche Hunt, was an attractive woman who never had to buy her own drinks at the Rovers. One September evening in 1974 she delighted in telling Annie, whom she felt needed taking down a peg or two, that they would soon be related; her 19-year-old daughter Deirdre had just agreed to marry Billy. When the would-be groom returned home that evening it was to the news that his mother had gone to bed early.

The next morning Annie attempted to ignore the fact that her plans for a society wedding for Billy had been ruined. Billy was infuriated by her lack of concern: "I'm waiting for you to say 'Congratulations Billy. You've found yourself a really nice girl at last.'"

Annie told him that it was obvious Deirdre wasn't a nice girl but a gold-digger pushed along by her grasping mother: "And they all grow like their mothers dear and Blanche Hunt puts me in mind of no one so much as Elsie Tanner." Annie spat out the last words with venom.

Billy refused to be put off Deirdre; he was adamant that at 36 he had the right to some happiness. Eventually Annie began to thaw towards the girl. With Lucille having gone to live in Ireland, the private quarters of the Rovers were empty at night apart from the Walkers. Annie grew to dislike the late evenings, after closing, when Billy would take Deirdre home and spend a few hours with her planning their future. After a couple of months Annie realised that unless she accepted Deirdre she faced a lonely future, alienated from her son.

However, as the wedding plans were carried forward into 1975, Deirdre decided she was too young to settle down and broke the engagement. Rather than being relieved, Annie was furious that her son had been dumped.

1974 ANNIE HAD FEARED THAT COMMON DEIRDRE WOULD BRING OUT THE WORST IN BILLY. SHE FELT VINDICATED WHEN, JUST DAYS INTO THEIR ENGAGEMENT, BILLY BRAWLED WITH RAY LANGTON OVER DEIRDRE.

— 1975 —

RATHER THAN HANG AROUND, tormented by the sight of Deirdre, whom he still loved, Billy left the Rovers and took a bar job in Jersey.

With Lucille and Billy gone, Annie was very much alone in the Rovers. Her days were filled with the bustle of coping with staff problems and serving customers, but at night, once the main door was bolted, she was quite alone. However, one November night, as she snuggled down under the bedclothes and smiled fondly at Jack's photograph, she was not alone. Two youths had hidden in the gents' toilet and, with the pub in darkness, crept out to see what they could steal from the living room. Far from your average delinquents, the lads were university educated, but unemployable as the recession bit hard.

One look at the regal landlady had convinced them that she had to have money stashed away, but after half an hour of turning out all the cupboards, Les and Neil were still empty-handed. It was then that they decided to tackle Annie in her bedroom and demand the money.

Annie was woken by her door opening and, pulling the light cord, she instinctively took control of the situation, ordering the lads out of her home. She grew angry when, ignoring her, Neil and Les started to root through her personal belongings demanding cash. Neil grew disgusted when all he found was costume jewellery: "Don't you even possess a watch? I mean, look at her. Ponced up like Barbara Cartland. She must have loads stashed away! Where is it? You've got it hidden away somewhere. So you can dip in. Buy yourself a face lift." Annie stood up to Neil; even when he threatened to harm her, she told him, quite rightly, that he did not have the nerve.

Les was the weaker of the two and Annie played on his sympathy, trying to engage him in conversation but he was too scared of Neil to take pity on her. Neil grew frantic with frustration as he failed to find anything of value in the pub. He even pulled the mattress off Annie's bed but failed to find any secret nest egg. Startled by the telephone ringing, Les pleaded with Neil to leave. Neil stopped himself from striking victorious Annie and the pair fled into the back yard, but they found their exit blocked. Albert Tatlock, next door at No.1, had been alarmed to hear the noises in the pub and had alerted builders Len Fairclough and Ray Langton. They arrived at the back door just as Neil and Les did. A vicious fight broke out which ended with Neil and Les running off, but not until Len and Ray had given them some bruises.

Annie, terribly shaken by the ordeal, fell down the stairs and ended up on the hall carpet. As she recovered she begged Len not to inform the brewery; she did not want them to think she was too vulnerable on her own to keep her licence.

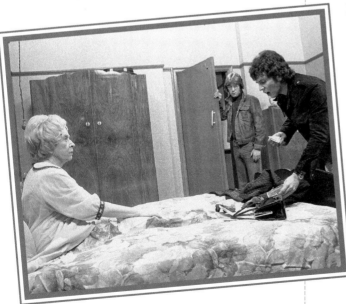

1975 ANNIE FACED A TERRIFYING ORDEAL WHEN YOUTHS THREATENED HER WITH VIOLENCE IN HER BEDROOM.

1976 BET AND BETTY WERE
AMUSED BY STAN'S ANTICS, BUT
HILDA WAS NOT: SHE HAD FEARED
HE WAS DEAD.

1976

ANNIE managed to keep the brewery in the dark about Les and Neil but they heard about a similar incident in early 1976. After the first ordeal, Annie had had locks fitted on all the doors and was able to rest easy in the knowledge that if anyone was lurking in the Gents they would not be able to get out.

One evening in March 1976, Bet had needed a barrel moved in the cellar, and Stan Ogden and Albert Tatlock had obliged her by shifting the barrel between them. Afterwards, they had taken the opportunity to look around the cellar and breathe in the wonderful smell of ale. While they were beneath ground Annie called time, cleared the pub and locked up.

When they first realised that they were locked in, Stan and Albert were startled at the thought of spending the night in the cellar, but they then realised that they were surrounded by barrels and barrels of glorious beer: "Come on, we must have been down 'ere half an hour. Annie Walker's had time to put her curlers up. Fancy a milk stout for starters? Can't beat it, can you. Locked in a pub cellar. You dream about summat like this happening to you." Albert settled down to work on the barrel of mild whilst Stan danced a jig and planned the night: "We'll stop down 'ere till we've had a few bevvies. Then we give Annie a shout. Tell her we've been shouting for yonks, and she's not heard us."

Whilst Hilda Ogden feared her Stan had left home or had met with a horrible accident, the two merry comrades whiled away the time by singing and cracking jokes. They soon fell into an argument over the different wars they had fought in, based not on battles fought but women won over. Albert reminisced about French girls, whilst Stan dreamed of an Italian lover.

At nine o'clock the next morning Bet was startled to hear cries from the cellar. She alerted Hilda and Annie and, armed with bottles, the women opened the cellar door. It was just in time for Albert: "Can't make me mind up what's worse. Busting to go to lavvy or facing Annie Walker." Annie was furious to find the men had helped themselves to drinks and had made no attempt to escape the cellar. Bet was incredulous: "What some folk'll do for a drink!"

The brewery heard of the story and told Annie there was no way she could continue to live in the pub alone. They ordered her to find a resident cellarman to replace Billy. The same day Fred Gee wandered into the pub having just been made redundant from a foundry and one of the Street's most unlikely partnerships was formed.

1977

ANNIE WALKER always prided herself on her judgement of character. Some of her regulars, such as social worker Ken Barlow, were treated as family members, and often invited into the living room for intellectual conversation. Others, such as layabout Eddie Yeats, were barely tolerated and Annie looked for any opportunity to bar them. In August 1977, Eddie cornered Annie and told her that he approved of the way she had had the pub decorated. He then turned on what he considered to be his charm and tried to sell her a unique carpet. Annie interrupted him: "Mr Yeats. Now, how can I say this without sounding too insulting? I wouldn't trust you – or your friends in the trade – as far as I could throw a hogshead of bitter." Eddie ignored the insult and plodded on, finally arousing Annie's curiosity by telling her the carpet he was offering would be monogrammed in gold.

One look at the interlocking A and W and Annie was smitten; she agreed to have the carpet fitted at £5 per yard. Once it was laid, Annie moved all the furniture to the walls so the green carpet with gold lettering could be shown off in all its glory. She was surprised that Eddie had been able to supply such a good quality carpet, but her cleaner Hilda Ogden knew exactly where it had come from and confided in Bet: "Just guess what Annie Walker and the Alhambra Weatherfield's got in common? That exclusive carpet of her's what was specially woven. From one end of the bingo hall to the other." Bet swore Hilda to secrecy, telling her they would find the right time to tell Duchess Annie. Fred Gee agreed: "When it comes to devious thinking, I've always rated Bet very high."

Bet, Fred and Hilda stood back and watched as, wanting to show off, Annie invited all the Lady Victuallers around for sherry. It was only

1977 BET AND HILDA DECIDED AGAINST REVEALING THE ORIGIN OF ANNIE'S CARPET UNTIL THEY HAD THE OPPORTUNITY TO THWART HER SOCIAL PRETENSIONS.

when the first couple were at the door that Bet delighted in dropping the bombshell that Annie's carpet was an off-cut of a bingo carpet: "If it stands stiletto heels and fag ends and the odd milk stout at a bingo hall, well, it ought to stand a bit of sherry." The staff watched as Annie's features creased into various expressions of horror, but it was too late to do anything but grin and bear it as the back-stabbing landladies tottered in. Annie prayed that none were bingo fanatics but unfortunately Estelle Plimpton was. After enduring an awful two hours of polite chit-chat and dodging the whispers and knowing smiles, Annie headed towards the bar to seek out a certain Mr Yeats.

1978

THE QUESTION OF ANNIE'S RETIREMENT raised its head again in May 1978. Annie had been away on holiday, this time visiting Billy in Jersey. She returned home to find that her car had been stolen and Fred had thrown an after-

hours party which the police had raided. The brewery were informed but were not too bothered as a rival company was attempting a takeover bid for the brewery. The news that Newton & Ridley might cease to trade was very upsetting to Annie; she grew concerned for her own future, realising that, at 69, she was only kept on out of sentiment. She became fraught with worry, prompting Betty Turpin to rally Billy and Joan together.

Annie was overjoyed to be visited by both of them, but after the initial welcome she let her mask slip and showed her fear for the future. Whilst Billy shared her concern, his sister did not want to get involved, fearing she'd be stuck with her mother if Annie was forced to leave the Rovers: "I think you're panicking. This whole stupid business is bound to blow over, you can see for yourself Mum's perfectly capable of carrying on as she is for a good few years yet."

Joan refused to acknowledge her mother's condition and wasn't in the room with Billy when Annie finally broke down into tears: "Whatever happens, whatever goes wrong in the end all the blame is laid at my door. All the responsibility. It's almost too much for me sometimes. It was so different when your poor, dear father..." Billy was stunned to see his mother so alone and put a protective arm around her. He realised that it was up to him to shoulder the responsibility to ensure his mother's peace of mind.

Annie's despair turned to delight when Billy announced that he had visited the brewery and had arranged to take over as landlord so they could run the pub together. Overcome with emotion and stunned by his generosity, Annie was speechless.

The next morning she admitted to having some doubts about the arrangement: "Even though you are my son, it won't be easy handing over. This has been my little kingdom, hasn't it? It's been my life." She realised that Billy would be giving up a lot – a good business and home in Jersey, friends and independence. The plans for Billy's takeover coincided with the news that Newton & Ridley was not being taken over and that Annie's position would be safe whatever happened.

Feeling years younger, Annie told Billy he couldn't have her pub any more. They were both relieved and Annie thanked her son for his willingness to sacrifice everything for her. As Billy headed back to Jersey, Annie treated herself to a week in a health farm.

1979

AFTER ENDING HER RELATIONSHIP with Billy Walker, Deirdre Hunt had married plumber Ray Langton. They had lived on the Street but the marriage had ended in 1978. Annie had watched Deirdre mature and blossom with the responsibility of motherhood. She had grown to respect the girl and often wondered what would have happened if Deirdre had married Billy. Annie had no grandchildren and took a particular interest in Deirdre's child Tracy. She was devastated in March 1979 when Tracy was feared dead after a lorry full of wood crashed into the Rovers.

1979 BILLY SWORE UNDYING LOVE TO DEIRDRE BUT ANNIE KNEW EXACTLY HOW TO TEAR THEM APART.

1980 ALWAYS KEEN ON PUBLIC ATTENTION, BET TOOK ADVANTAGE OF THE BIN STRIKE TO GET HER PICTURE IN THE PAPER.

When Tracy was found alive, Annie, along with the other residents, was delighted.

However, no matter how fond she was of Deirdre and the child she was not willing to see Billy become involved with them. Billy turned up in the Summer of 1979 in deep financial trouble. He needed £2,500 to start up a new venture, a partnership in a wine bar. Annie was annoyed that he had visited only because he needed money, and she became worried as he seemed to be taking an interest in Deirdre once again. Annie was even more against the match than she had been in 1974: Deirdre was now a separated woman, with a child. Billy told her she was just being old fashioned: "There's nothing to stop 'er gettin' a divorce. An' yeah,

she's got a kid, so what? I thought you always wanted a grandchild." Annie was appalled by the suggestion: "One of my own blood, yes. Not Ray Langton's child!"

Annie accused Deirdre of being desperate for a man to support her and Tracy and told Billy she would not let him be a fool. He was stunned when she gave him a choice – Deirdre or the £2,500. For all his talk of loving Deirdre and enjoying being with Tracy, when it came down to it, Billy wanted the wine bar more than anything and, just as Annie had hoped, he told Deirdre he would not be marrying her.

Billy left for Jersey with a cheque in his pocket, leaving Deirdre behind to be consoled by Ken Barlow. Two years later Annie attended Deirdre and Ken's wedding, relieved that Deirdre was no longer a threat.

1980

LOCAL BINMEN EDDIE YEATS AND JOHNNY WEBB caused an uproar in October 1980 and deeply offended Annie. They had no intention of being offensive, they just thought they were being helpful by returning a half-empty can of hair dye to the landlady across the bar, explaining she had thrown it away, obviously by mistake. Annie was furious: "What I put into my dustbin is between me and my Maker and nobody else's business." She threw the pair out of the pub when Eddie told everyone her hair was dyed Platinum Pearl.

She complained to the Council and demanded another crew to clear her rubbish. This offended the binmen and Annie suddenly discovered her bins had been blacked with a threatened strike if any crew touched them.

After a week, the pile of binbags spilled over the Rovers' yard and the smell caused the customers to insist that Annie sort out the disagreement. Annie refused to back down without an apology from Eddie, annoying even her closest friends, like grocer Alf Roberts: "If you'll take my advice, Annie, you'll climb down off your high horse, because when it comes to things as can bring rats it's no laughing matter!"

Annie paid window cleaner Stan Ogden to take the rubbish to the Council tip in his cart, but the binmen saw him and threatened him with violence if he touched the bags. In desperation, Annie ordered Fred to load her precious Rover 2000 with the bins but he was turned back from the tip by the binmen who recognised him. To the astonishment of the barstaff Annie announced that the whole business was bringing on a migraine, and she would have to visit Joan in Derby. She left, telling them to sort the rubbish situation out.

The smell of the rotting rubbish lured the local press to the Rovers, eager for a human-interest story. The Gazette photographer snapped photographs of Bet sitting amongst the rubbish in her tightest skirt, while a reporter jotted down the facts. A week later the brewery contacted Annie in Derby after reading about the situation. She stormed home to confront her staff: "'Blonde, attractive Miss Lynch said: 'It's a storm in a teacup really. If

both parties had behaved with a bit of common sense in the first place it would never have come to this.' I consider this to be a gross betrayal." Annie threatened to sack her staff and forced them to apologise to her.

Annie herself was forced to apologise to the binmen after telling herself that it was her duty to do so: "It needs one of the parties to be wise and intelligent enough to stop this dispute. Perhaps I should apologise to those stupid binmen. For the country's sake, we don't want another winter of discontent, do we?"

1981

CASABLANCA beckoned Annie in March 1981. She set off on a three-week cruise, leaving the pub in the hands of temporary manager Gordon Lewis. Bet, Betty and Fred were very put out as Annie told them she was being forced to bring a manager in because she could not trust them: "With Mr Lewis here to look after things there's less chance of the police investigating us for serving drinks after hours or Bet gracing the papers of the Gazette posing on a pile of rubbish. Do I make myself clear?" Annie left the pub confident that Gordon would firmly control the staff. She returned three weeks

1981 GORDON LEWIS UPSET THE STAFF BY TAKING CONTROL OF THE PUB AND CRITICISING THEM AT EVERY OPPORTUNITY. BET AND BETTY WALKED OUT WHEN HE SUSPENDED FRED.

1982 BET AND BETTY WERE NOT IMPRESSED WHEN FRED'S ANTICS AT THE BALL CAUSED ANNIE TO RETIRE TO BED WITH A MIGRAINE.

later to discover that his rod of iron had been so firm that Fred was suspended and Bet and Betty had walked out in support.

Gordon enjoyed his time at the Rovers, once he had got rid of the riff-raff behind the bar. He was furious when Annie reinstated them all but she told him it was nothing to do with him: "One thing I have learned, over many years in the licensed trade, is the value of keeping a reliable staff." Gordon refused to back down, and, telling Annie that she was too set in her ways, he challenged her claim that he had a lot to learn: "Well, Newton & Ridley don't seem to agree with you. They're looking for a house for me. To be quite frank, Mrs Walker, I wouldn't be surprised if they put me in here when you decided to call it a day." He felt he had handled the situation well, but was stunned when Annie informed him that Mr Cresswell had asked her to write a report on him. Annie assured him that she had told the brewery exactly what she had thought of him.

1982

THE 200TH ANNIVERSARY of Newton & Ridley, Stag Brewery, fell in January 1982. To mark the occasion, the brewery threw a lavish ball, inviting all their landlords and landladies. Annie planned the evening weeks in advance, wanting to create the right impression. However, her plans were thrown into confusion when her escort backed out because of illness. She refused to go alone and was forced to accept the only available man at short notice – Fred Gee.

The next morning Bet told him she was proud of him: "That a lad from the spit an' sawdust end of the trade could be in there, what you might call 'mingling' with the top brass. Makes yer think."

Fred could remember little of the evening, except that he had danced with Sarah Ridley. He chortled at the memory: "Foxtrottin' there with a brewery heiress." Annie, however, remembered every terrible moment: "Being escorted by Fred was rather like being escorted by a very low, vulgar comedian." She tried hard to forget about the night's events, but unfortunately Fred had made that impossible. At the ball he had chatted to salesmen and told everyone the Rovers was his pub. He had also left the Rover 2000 somewhere but couldn't remember where.

Annie was relieved when the car was traced, but became concerned when a van delivered a noisy Space Invaders machine, ordered by

Fred. The customers enjoyed it but Annie hated the noise and pulled the plug. A car salesman turned up next with Mr Gee's new Rover limousine, which he had requested to test drive. Bet thought the situation was hilarious: "Bung the Space Invaders in the boot of the limo. An' maybe – if you talk to him nicely – this fancy dealer – he'll drop you off at the Job Centre."

Fred spent a day sweating and finally told the salesman he didn't want the car. Bet put in another cruel jibe: "Fred, what's full of little green men and goes at 150 miles an hour?... An E-type Space Invaders machine."

Fred assured Annie that there would be no more deliveries, unaware that at that very moment Miss Phyllis Lomax was in the bar waiting to see Mr Gee. Bet struggled to keep a straight face as Phyllis – a waitress from the ball – told bewildered Fred that she had come to view his little haunt. She reminded him that he had offered her a job as head waitress at his restaurant. He managed to convince her that she must have mistaken him for someone else and she left, disappointed. Fred was relieved that Annie had not caught him posing as the boss.

1983

OVER THE NEXT YEAR Fred had many chances to pretend he was the boss as Annie's health deteriorated and she spent more time away from the bar. She eventually moved away to live in Derby, retiring from the licensed trade, but that was not before she had to spend an evening coping behind the bar alone when the staff had failed to appear for opening time.

It was a sunny Bank Holiday and Fred had taken Bet and Betty for a trip in the country in the Rover 2000. Unfortunately, the brakes were faulty and when Fred slammed the boot after a picnic, the car started to roll down a hill, picking up speed until it came to rest with a crash in a huge lake. This would have been disastrous enough but the situation was made worse by the fact that Bet and Betty were in the car at the time. The handbrake had come off in Bet's hand as she had pulled at it: "I never bought a flag this year, for the lifeboats. D'yer think I'm being punished?"

The water was freezing and whilst Fred worried about the car, Bet and Betty grew concerned about how they were to get back to dry land. Betty, in the back seat, was grateful there were no sharks around, but she was anxious to get free: "If my knees get chilled I'll be crippled." Bet refused to get her outfit wet and ordered Fred to carry her to safety on his back. Her state of mind was not helped when, having reached the shore, he dumped her down like a sack of coals: "Frederick, my boy. Things were bad. You had more than enough to answer for. But now you have put the top hat on things with a vengeance. You have done me and my

1983 A QUIET DAY IN THE COUNTRY
ENDED WITH A PLUNGE IN A LAKE FOR BET AND BETTY.

gorgeous new outfit the final, unforgivable mischief. Not content with tryin' your damndest to feed me to the fishes, you have put me down right slap bang in the middle of a cow plop!"

1984

"ME MOTHER'S BOWING OUT. From now on it's going to be my name on the licence. And my name over that door". The staff at The Rovers Return were not surprised that Annie had decided to give up the pub but they were not happy at the prospect of having sombre Billy as their new boss. Over the years, Billy had fallen foul of various money-making schemes, befriended some very shady characters, and he was a hard task master. He, also, was not very happy at the prospect of running the "battered old boozer"; he had been forced to take it on in order to pay off a £6,000 debt he had acquired in Jersey. However, he decided to make the most of his lot and skim as much profit as he could from the Rovers.

Billy's first decision was to sack Fred Gee, whom he considered idle and worthless. Rather than pay him redundancy for his years of service, Billy tolerated his presence whilst

treating him as a skivvy until Fred was goaded into hitting him. Billy did not mind the black eye he was left with as it meant Fred could be, and was, instantly dismissed without redundancy payment. Billy relied heavily on Bet and Betty to run the bar, while he and his flash friends spent the takings at the races during the day and the casino at nights.

Billy was never a good gambler and he lost heavily during these days of fun and frivolity. To boost the pub's profit margins, and therefore his own wallet, Billy stopped buying his spirits from the brewery, as he was contracted to do. Instead, he visited the wholesalers and stocked the cellar with cheap spirits. Betty, a policeman's widow, was worried about the pub's reputation with the brewery and asked him to tow the line. He ignored her. She also worried when Billy started to throw parties after hours, encouraging the regulars to stay and buy more drinks at a special rate. Again Billy ignored Betty's warnings and paid the price when the pub was raided by the police. Everyone present had to give their names to the police. Unfortunately Jack Duckworth panicked and told the police he was

1984 BILLY AND HIS FRIENDS USED THE ROVERS AS THEIR OWN SOCIAL CLUB UNTIL THE LOCAL POLICE CAUGHT THEM OUT. BILLY TRIED TO WIN THE POLICE ROUND, SAYING HIS MOTHER HAD BEEN MAYORESS, BUT THE POLICE WERE UNMOVED.

1985 RELAXING AWAY FROM CORONATION STREET - LANDLADY BET SOAKS IN THE BLACKPOOL SUN WITH MATES RITA FAIRCLOUGH AND MAVIS RILEY.

Stan Ogden, unaware that Stan had died in hospital that very night.

Sarah Ridley summoned Billy to her office at the brewery and told him she was not happy with his behaviour. Billy grew angry at her interference: "It's not easy making a living in a little back-street pub in this part of the world. It's not exactly Silicon Valley round here, you know. More like Death Valley." Miss Ridley did not like Billy running down Weatherfield and the pub that his own mother had cherished for more than 40 years. When she told him the brewery regretted giving him the tenancy he said the feeling was mutual and asked her to buy him out: "Tradition's all very well. But it can smother you if you're not careful". Miss Ridley and Mr Walker toasted the end of the Walker era and the next day Billy sped off back to Jersey, leaving an uncertain future at The Rovers Return.

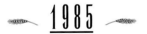

1985

SARAH RIDLEY MOVED QUICKLY to fill the gap left by Billy at the Rovers. The brewery decided to appoint a manager rather than sell the pub to another tenant who might prove as unsuitable as Billy. The regulars at the Rovers were reluctant to have the harmony of the pub disrupted by an outsider and pushed Bet Lynch into applying for the job. Then, behind her back, they sent Sarah a petition supporting the barmaid's appointment.

Bet was stunned when she was given the job of manageress – Newton & Ridley's first single manageress – and the regulars were delighted. Mike Baldwin toasted her with champagne: "This is a rough old pub and it needs a rough old bird in charge of it."

The transformation from brassy barmaid to respectable manageress was a hard one for Bet to make. She moved into the living quarters at the Rovers – her first real home in her life – and kept a framed photograph of Annie Walker on the fireplace to remind her constantly of the great lady. Her rise in income allowed more classy outfits and led to the demise of the outrageous earrings that had become her trade mark, though her taste remained flamboyant.

A three-week training course added managerial skills to her experience behind the bar, and a new staff – Gloria Todd and Jack Duckworth – helped her to cope with the frightening responsibility she now held. The local landladies, led by bitchy Stella Rigby, roped her in for social evenings and nights on the town and slowly Bet realised she had to tread carefully with boyfriends if she was to avoid upsetting the brewery.

She nearly lost her job in the Spring of 1985 when she went on a Norwegian cruise with barman Frank Mills, giving the pub keys to Hilda Ogden and asking her to inform the brewery. Unfortunately, Hilda did not hear the latter request and the staff were left to wonder about Bet's absence. When Bet returned, two weeks later, it was to find Betty had been made manager and that she had been put on probation by a brewery that no longer trusted her. The probation period lasted three months and during that time Bet kept her head down and the profits up, winning her permanent job back in the end.

1986

THE FIRE THAT GUTTED THE ROVERS in June 1986 also threatened to destroy Bet Lynch's emotions. For 16 years she had worked at the pub, which was now her only achievement in life. Sometimes she had pulled pints with smiles that had hidden tears, but she had never dropped the cheerful facade that had made her so popular with the regulars. The Rovers had been more than a building; it was her life and her home: "When I first come 'ere to the Rovers, it was first time in me life I felt I'd found somewhere I really belonged. Jobs came an' went, fellers came an' went. But at this old dump, I found summat to 'ang on to. Not just a job, but a place where Bet Lynch finally amounted to summat. I s'pose what it give me was some self respect."

Bet had left the Rovers with nothing but a nightgown and a plastic bag containing a fake leopard-skin coat, a singed wig and a pair of shoes. She felt she had no future left. Suddenly everything changed, the bleakness dispelled by a ray of sunshine from the brewery. Her spirits rose when she was told that the gutted building was not to be pulled down but rebuilt and refurbished. The brewery kept her on the payroll during the months of rebuilding and she was consulted over furniture, decoration and new staff.

It was a new Bet who flung open the doors to the new Rovers on 13 August 1988. Hilda Ogden, as the pub's longest-serving member of staff, performed the opening ceremony and was given a tour of the new pub by Bet: "Have a good look at it Hilda, the way it looks now, all clean and lovely. That's the way I want it every morning. So think on."

For Bet, the nightmare of the Rovers' fire had been replaced by the satisfaction of seeing the old pub given a facelift it and its regulars truly

1986 HILDA PERFORMED THE REOPENING CEREMONY AT THE ROVERS IN AUGUST. SHE KNEW BEER-BELLIED STAN WOULD HAVE BEEN PROUD OF HER.

deserved. The only person who was unhappy about the reopened pub was Alec Gilroy, manager of the Graffiti Club, who had done a roaring trade while the Rovers' had been closed. With the pub back on its feet the Graffiti was empty again. Alec Gilroy was not a happy man.

1987

ON THE DAY OF THE ROVERS' reopening Bet had been a very happy sunbeam. Six months later, in the Spring of 1987, the novelty of running a fancy new bar was replaced by the monotony of serving the same faces, and the pressure piled on by the brewery to push the profits up more and more. Bet fell into a depression as, no matter what scheme she started – cabaret evenings, happy hours – the brewery were never satisfied with her takings. A lot of money had been spent on the pub and they were looking for a handsome return.

Bet knew that she had to break the chain

that was making her life so miserable. Envying Annie Walker's freedom, she considered buying the tenancy and was then forced into doing so by the brewery, which introduced a new policy whereby managers had to either buy the tenancies or move out. Bet needed to raise £15,000 quickly. In desperation she turned to Alec Gilroy, who had once offered her financial support if it was needed. He agreed to lend the money and she agreed to pay it back at 10% interest. Bet celebrated the fact that she now owned the pub and was free to do with it whatever she wanted. She soon discovered that she was no better off; she was simply slaving away for herself rather than someone else, without the benefit of a regular pay cheque at the end of the week. She grew concerned about her repayments to Alec and, fearing she would suffer the humiliation of losing the pub, she packed a bag and fled.

The brewery were alerted to Bet's absence and, worried about his investment, Alec ordered an investigation. The brewery agreed to make him temporary manager so he could keep an eye on his money. Three months passed before Bet contacted the brewery to say she was in Spain. Alec immediately flew out to track her down. He found her working in a café in Torremolinos and demanded to know the fate of the £2,000 of his money she still had.

She explained that his money was safe, but she had nothing left: "My future's all mapped out. I'll get a job behind a bar somewhere and be a barmaid till I drop, or my feet give out. Working for somebody else the rest of my life."

Seeing her destitute Alec realised how strong his feelings were for Bet and he proposed marriage, explaining that she could still control the pub if she were his wife. To her surprise – and to the surprise of her friends back home – Bet agreed. A month later she became Mrs Alec Gilroy.

Alec was given the licence of the pub and, as a wedding present he told Bet the bar was hers. Bet was back in charge.

1988 AFTER MISCARRYING HER BABY, BET BOUNCED BACK AND TOOK IN AN ALSATIAN, ROVER, MUCH TO THE ALARM OF DOG-HATER ALEC. HE PAID A LITTLE BOY TO CLAIM ROVER AS HIS LOST PET.

1988

BET SOON SETTLED DOWN to married life, a situation she had dreamed of for over 40 years but which had eluded her hitherto. She attempted to be the ideal wife, giving up the bar to concentrate on cooking wholesome meals for hubby, but after sampling her cooking Alec asked her to stop: "Forget all this little housewife stuff. Comb your hair, put some lipstick on and come and stand looking knockout behind that bar, where you belong."

Having got Bet out of the kitchen and on display in the pub, Alec found it hard to watch her in operation, flirting with the customers to boost profits. He sincerely loved her and he grew jealous of her relationship with the customers. However, to Bet it was just part of the job: "Can't you understand, Alec, that being chatted up is what you call an occupational hazard for a barmaid. And, let's be honest, a very enjoyable hazard. But that doesn't mean just cos I'm enjoyin' it that I'm makin' secret arrangements to go hoppin' into bed with somebody." She was touched when Alec admitted, for the first time, that he was jealous: "I suppose it all boils down to the fact I still can't believe me luck. That somebody like you could even be bothered with a bloke like me."

The Gilroy's happiness was cemented by Bet's news, in March 1988, that she was pregnant. At first Alec felt he was too old for

fatherhood but the idea soon grew on him when Bet reminded him of the night she had conceived: "There were a full moon. You kept leaping about saying you felt immortal. I thought it was the half bottle of brandy you'd supped. But it must have bin the sap rising."

The Gilroys planned for the future of their baby, both having missed out so much on their own children growing up – Bet's son had been adopted at six weeks, Alec's daughter had been brought up by his estranged first wife. However, tragedy struck a week later when Bet miscarried. Returning from hospital, Alec tried to get ashen-faced Bet to rest for a few days, but she refused. Staggering to her feet she hugged him and told him she'd be in the bar as soon as she'd put her face on: "We've got a pub to open in five minutes. That's what we do kid, you and me. Run a pub. Let's get on with it."

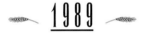

1989

AS WELL AS RUNNING THE ROVERS, Alec Gilroy continued to hold onto his theatrical agency. He had over 50 acts on his books and coped with the stress of a day at the Rovers by spending evenings taking in the clubs, checking on his acts. In March 1989, Alec was given the chance to take some of his acts on a tour of the Middle East. The pay was too good to give up, especially as he had a heavy tax bill to pay.

Bet was not keen on the idea of running the pub alone for three months but Alec convinced her they needed the money. She agreed to his going but quickly changed her mind when he signed up his first act – attractive snake-dancing Tanya: "I can just see you and her out there in the Middle East on them hot sultry nights – being warm-hearted and impulsive together." Alec was adamant that Tanya was a good,

1989 ALEC WAS DELIGHTED TO SEE WELSH MEGAN BUT BET WAS NOT IMPRESSED WITH TALES OF HER PERFORMING SNAKES AND BUDGIES.

wholesome girl who had given the snake up in favour of budgies: "She's not really called Tanya. Her real name's Megan Morgan. Her Dad had a pet shop in Merthyr Tydfil." Alec maintained it was in their interests for him to take the tour and left.

Throughout their married life, Bet and Alec spent many months away from each other. This tour was to be the first of many, with Alec flying all over the world whilst Bet struggled on at the pub. This contentious issue finally led to their separation, with Alec leaving to oversee theatrical acts on cruise ships for Sunglobe Cruises.

1990

"I CAN JUST SEE IT. Peephole in the door, piano player in the corner and 'Studs' Gilroy in a black shirt and white tie moving around exchanging witty conversation with the local hoods."

1990 REGULARS MIKE BALDWIN AND DES BARNES WERE FORCED TO USE THE ROVERS' BACK ENTRANCE DURING THE LOCK-OUT.

do anything to keep the Rovers as it was. Telling Nigel to stick his plans, the couple locked themselves in the pub, serving faithful regulars via the back door. When Nigel tried to enter the pub, Bet beat him about the head with her stuffed snake draught excluder and threw him out: "I've forgot more manners than you'll ever have, you great poncified streak of aerated gnat's water!"

The local radio station picked up the story and some of the regulars urged the brewery to change their plans. Ridley stuck firm and the Gilroys were told to vacate the pub as the brewery were repossessing it. The Gilroys remained dignified to the end, refusing to lose their composure in front of the brewery bosses. Nigel Ridley took the pub off the Gilroys and was in the middle of evicting them when Cecil Newton arrived to put a stop to the nonsense: "Nobody's going to be wearing cowboy hats and selling fire water in The Rovers Return while I'm alive. The Rovers stays as it is. A working-man's pub where working men live."

Nigel was given his marching orders and the pub was reprieved. Bet swore that no one would touch the structure of the pub whilst she was around to defend it.

Bet Gilroy was scathing in her response to the news that brewery new boy Nigel Ridley had decided to turn the Rovers into a Bronx bar. Alec was keen on the idea and enjoyed the image conjured up by his wife. However, Bet left him in no doubt at all regarding her feelings: "I'll tell you what's wrong with it, Mr Capone. I like it the way it is!"

Nigel's plans were complex; they involved buying No. 1 from Deirdre Barlow and knocking through from the pub. Bet was alarmed as Nigel explained the new arrangements: "Your present accommodation will be the new Bronx Bar and Carvery... Your turnover will be increased four hundred per cent. Of course you'll have an increased work load and we'd expect you to stay open all day, so you'll need extra staff." Even Alec grew concerned as Nigel outlined the higher rent and harder work involved. The Gilroys were then given the choice: take on the revamped Rovers – or "Yankees" as it would be called – or take over The Quarryman's Rest. Alec was shaken to the core: "Dingiest, most miserable spot in God's creation. And I mean ,what trade does it get? There's only the cemetery trade."

The prospect of running a ghost pub united the Gilroys, and Bet took a stand, saying she'd

1991

ON THE AFTERNOON of 19 July 1991 Alec Gilroy's life changed forever. A policeman called at the pub to break the news that Alec's daughter Sandra and her husband Tim Arden had both been killed in a car crash. There was only an hour to go before the train bringing their daughter Victoria back from school was due to arrive in

Manchester, so Alec had to bottle up his grief in order to meet the train and then break the news to the 14-year-old girl that she was an orphan.

Alec was appointed Vicky's legal guardian and the Gilroys were thrown into emotional upheaval as they came to terms with having a dependant teenager, the first to live at the Rovers since Lucille Hewitt.

Vicky struggled to adjust to leaving her expensive Cheshire home to live in a poky room over a back-street pub: "I can't see anything from the windows except the opposite side of the street. Everything's so ugly. I don't like the smell of beer or the smell of cigarette smoke."

Bet was forced to stand back and bite her tongue as she watched Alec's bumbling attempts to win Vicky over and the girl's outright contempt for her grandfather's efforts. Eventually, after a month of turmoil, Vicky discovered a reason to enjoy Weatherfield. It came in the shape of Steve McDonald from No.11. The pair started dating and when she had to return to school, Vicky looked forward to the holidays when they could be together again.

1992

SHORTLY BEFORE ALEC bid farewell to the Rovers and Bet, one of his uncharitable acts set in chain a course of events that led to the complete refurbishment of the pub's cooking facilities. For years Betty had cooked in the Rovers' kitchen, serving up hotpot and soup for the customers. When needed, for occasions such as weddings and parties, Betty could run to sandwiches and trifle but the majority of her culinary skills were reserved for the lunch-time trade.

Alec had refused to re-employ barmaid Liz McDonald after she had left to have a baby. Her husband Jim grew angry at the way Alec had treated her and, to get his own back, led Alec to believe that he had reported him to the Health Inspector for preparing bar food in a domestic kitchen. Fearing an investigation, Alec promptly stopped the bar food and sacked Betty, explaining to Bet that she was only useful for preparing food. Betty was furious at being cast aside after 23 years of faithful service: "You've hurt me, Alec. I've been a loyal employee to you, and a good friend to Bet all these years."

Bet made Alec see that the profits would be cut if they didn't continue with food, and all that was needed was for the kitchen to be modernised to reach the standards required by the Environmental Health regulations. Alec reluctantly saw the sense in the argument and also agreed to re-employ Betty: "There's no getting rid of her, is there? She should be written into the deeds of this place."

Coincidentally, just as Betty was returning to work, the Environmental Health officer was learning of the goings on at the pub. He had no record of a complaint being brought against the Rovers but was interested to hear of how

1992 JIM TOOK BETTY'S HOTPOT AS EVIDENCE AGAINST
ALEC, BUT HIS JOKE BACKFIRED WHEN BETTY WAS SACKED.

1993

IN SEPTEMBER 1992 Alec left the Rovers to start a new life in Southampton, leaving Bet alone at the pub. It had been her decision to stay as she could not bring herself to leave the pub that had become her life, her career and her home. However, Alec had already sold the tenancy back to the brewery so Bet could only hang on to the pub as manageress. She found it difficult to adjust to not owning the pub or the furniture which used to be hers. The new brewery manager, Richard Willmore, is a hard task master, pushing Bet to make more and more profits. She has had to throw an extended Happy Hour – running from 5 to 6.30 pm – and has had to suffer the humiliation of seeing her own protégé Liz McDonald moved into her own, upmarket pub. But Bet hangs onto the Rovers' crown, with the help of Betty who has been the backbone of the pub for a quarter of a century. There are bound to be more fights on the horizon, more challenges and more dramas, but whilst Bet and Betty are serving behind the bar customers will always be guaranteed a warm welcome, quick service and a great dollop of hotpot!

quickly Alec had sacked Betty. He decided to check out the Rovers himself. He caught Alec out in the middle of the lunch-time rush and was not impressed by what he found in the kitchen: "Cracked tiles...flaking emulsion paint on the ceiling...a washing machine. That means dirty clothes, means contamination. Means it can't stay in kitchen. And the coat behind the door – people could have spat on it without you knowing." Betty was not charmed by this thought, and Alec was horrified as the officer closed the kitchen down and gave him three weeks to have the £7,000 alterations carried out. Three weeks and a huge dent in Alec's wallet later, the Rovers reopened for food. To see a quicker return on his money, Alec decided to serve food in the evenings as well, laying on a larger selection of dishes. Betty refused to work evenings so Liz McDonald was brought back to serve curries, lasagne and chips.

1993 GIVING BET THEIR FULL SUPPORT, THE ROVERS' STAFF FACE THE FUTURE.

CAST LIST

THOSE WHO SERVED:

Maureen Barnett..........................Maureen Morris
Suzie Birchall..........................Cheryl Murray
Charlie Bracewell ....Peter Bayliss
Amy Burton...............................Fanny Carby
Carole..................................Greta Schmidt
Ivan Cheveski...........................Ernst Walder
Diane...................................Lottie Ward
Alison Dougherty ....Elizabeth Ritson
Jack Duckworth..........................William Tarmey
Jacko Ford..............................Robert Keegan
Tina Fowler.............................Michelle Holmes
Angie Freeman...........................Deborah McAndrew
Fred Gee................................Fred Feast
Alec Girloy.............................Roy Barraclough
Bet Gilroy, nee Lynch...................Julie Goodyear
Kath Goodwin ....Lori Wells Keefe
Frank Harvey............................Nick Stringer
Concepta Hewitt, nee Riley..............Doreen Keogh
Lucille Hewitt..........................Jennifer Moss
Arlene Jones............................Geraldine Moffatt
Sam Leach...............................Frank Atkinson
Gordon Lewis............................David Daker
Martha Longhurst ....Lynne Carol
Doreen Lostock..........................Angela Crow
Liz McDonald ....Beverley Callard
Frank Mills.............................Nigel Gregory
Emily Nugent ....Eileen Derbyshire
Hilda Ogden.............................Jean Alexander
Irma Ogden.............................Sandra Gough
Dawn Perks.............................Jeanette Wild
Vince Plummer ....Garfield Morgan
Gail Potter............................Helen Worth
Margo Richardson ....Vicky Ogden
Brenda Riley...........................Eileen Kennally
Sally Seddon...........................Sally Whittaker
Wilf Starkey...........................Jim Bywater
Sandra Stubbs..........................Sally Watts
Glyn Thomas............................Alan David
Gloria Todd............................Sue Jenkins
Betty Turpin...........................Betty Driver
Annie Walker...........................Doris Speed
Arthur Walker..........................Jack Allen
Billy Walker...........................Kenneth Farrington
Jack Walker............................Arthur Leslie
Nona Willis............................Barbara Ferris
Raquel Wolstenhulme ....Sarah Lancashire

FROM THE TRADE:

Nellie Harvey ....Mollie Sugden
Richard Cresswell......................Timothy Carlton
Cecil Newton ....Kenneth Alan Taylor
George Newton ....Michael Browning
Anita Reynolds ....Elisabeth Sladen
Nigel Ridley ....John Basham
Sarah Ridley...........................Carole Nimmons
Stella Rigby...........................Vivienne Ross
Richard Willmore.......................Oliver Beamish

FEATURED REGULARS:

Victoria Arden ....Chloe Newsome
Mike Baldwin...........................Johnny Briggs
Deirdre Barlow, nee Hunt...............Anne Kirkbride
Frank Barlow ....Frank Pemberton
Ken Barlow ....William Roache
Des Barnes ....Philip Middlemiss
Jenny Bradley..........................Sally Ann Matthews
Minnie Caldwell ....Margot Bryant
Terry Duckworth........................Nigel Pivaro
Vera Duckworth ....Elizabeth Dawn
Len Fairclough ....Peter Adamson
Rita Fairclough ....Barbara Knox
Audrey Fleming ....Gillian McCann
Neil Fox ....Terence Budd
Dot Greenhalgh ....Joan Francis
Les Grimes ....Mike Grady
Charles Halliday.......................Anthony Booth
Harry Hewitt ....Ivan Beavis
Jim McDonald ....Charles Lawson
Megan Morgan ....Sue Roderick
Stan Ogden ....Bernard Youens
Rev Rawlinson ....Jeffrey Gardiner
Mavis Riley ....Thelma Barlow
Alf Roberts ....Bryan Mosley
Renee Roberts..........................Madge Hindle
Ena Sharples ....Violet Carson
Percy Sugden...........................Bill Waddington
Leonard Swindley ....Arthur Lowe
Dennis Tanner ....Philip Lowrie
Elsie Tanner ....Patricia Phoenix
Albert Tatlock ....Jack Howarth
Frank Turner ....Tom Watson
Joan Walker ....June Barry and Dorothy White
Kevin Webster ....Michael Le Vell
Ethne Willoughby.......................Barbara Lott

OTHER TV DRAMA SERIAL TITLES AVAILABLE FROM BOXTREE:

1–85283–480–3	Soldier, Soldier	£9.99
1–85283–474–9	Heartbeat: The Real Life Story	£14.99
1–85283–926–0	Taggart Casebook	£14.99
1–85283–946–5	Brookside: Life In The Close	£14.99
1–85283–922–8	Emmerdale Family Album	£13.99
1–85283–911–2	The Bill: The First Ten Years	£14.99
1–85283–471–4	On Call With Doctor Finlay	£9.99
0–7522–0984–1	Between The Lines	£9.99
0–7522–0974–4	Cracker	£9.99

All these books are available at your local bookshop or newsagent, or can be ordered direct from the publisher. Just tick the titles you want and fill in the form below.

Prices and availability subject to change without notice.

Boxtree Cash Sales, P.O. Box 11, Falmouth, Cornwall TR10 9EN.

Please send cheque or postal order for the value of the book, and add the following for postage and packing:

U.K. including B.F.P.O. £1.00 for one book, plus 50p for the second book, and 30p for each additional book ordered up to a £3.00 maximum.

OVERSEAS INCLUDING EIRE – £2.00 for the first book, plus £1.00 for the second book, and 50p for each additional book ordered.

OR Please debit this amount from my Access/Visa Card (delete as appropriate).

Card Number ....

Amount £ ....

Valid From Date ....

Expiry Date ....

Signed ....

Cardholder's Name ....

Cardholder's Address ....

Delivery Address (if different from above) ....

....